Matthieu looked at her reproachfully

"After all my efforts at saving you from the pressing attentions of Jeffrey Vane! I might just as well not have bothered, for all the thanks I'm getting."

"What were you expecting?" Her eyes challenged his. "A five-minute speech, or a framed testimonial for chivalry?"

"No, just this—the nicest reward of all." He caught her against him and bent his head. His mouth came down on hers, his lips cool at first, then warming. Rosamond felt as if time were suspended.

He lifted his mouth after a while and said against her lips, "Don't you think it's nice, too? Don't you want to prolong this? Be honest, Rosamond Briarley."

Her eyes met his candidly. "I think I'll admit I do—I'm not made of marble—but I don't really think it's wise!"

New Zealand born **Essie Summers** comes from a long line of storytellers. At eighteen she submitted her writing for publication and soon saw her poems, articles and short stories in print. Essie Summers debuted as a Harlequin author in 1961, has more than forty books to her credit and, as readers around the world will confirm, is one of the best-loved writers.

Books by Essie Summers

HARLEQUIN ROMANCE

2000—NOT BY APPOINTMENT
2021—BEYOND THE FOOTHILLS
2068—GOBLIN HILL
2133—ADAIR OF STARLIGHT PEAKS
2148—SPRING IN SEPTEMBER
2281—MY LADY OF THE FUCHSIAS
2322—ONE MORE RIVER TO CROSS
2453—THE TENDER LEAVES
2525—DAUGHTER OF THE MISTY GORGES
2590—A MOUNTAIN FOR LUENDA
2622—A LAMP FOR JONATHAN
2645—SEASON OF FORGETFULNESS
2688—WINTER IN JULY
2766—TO BRING YOU JOY

These books may be available at your local bookseller.

Don't miss any of our special offers. Write to us at the following address for information on our newest releases.

Harlequin Reader Service
901 Fuhrmann Blvd., P.O. Box 1397, Buffalo, NY 14240
Canadian address: P.O. Box 603,
Fort Erie, Ont. L2A 9Z9

Autumn in April
Essie Summers

Harlequin Books

TORONTO • NEW YORK • LONDON
AMSTERDAM • PARIS • SYDNEY • HAMBURG
STOCKHOLM • ATHENS • TOKYO • MILAN

Original hardcover edition published in 1981
by Mills & Boon Limited

ISBN 0-373-02801-6

Harlequin Romance first edition November 1986

For my daughter, Elizabeth,
who shared with me in 1972
the delights of the Isle of Wight,
whence our forebears came,
and for her husband, Robert,
who shares with her their
New Zealand world of farm and lake.

So many of my readers come to New Zealand as tourists and take pleasure in visiting the spots I use as settings in my books that I feel that I should mention that in this one, as in *The Gold of Noon* and *The Lake of the Kingfisher*, I made Moana-Kotare an imaginary lake for the purposes of the stories concerned. But it could be any of the colourful lakes of Central Otago, and in my mind's eyes, and in yours, I hope, it lies with its shimmering blue-green waters somewhere between Queenstown and Arrowtown.

CHAPTER ONE

ROSAMOND knew this was the best fashion show she'd ever compered for Dellabridges. This one was all hers. She'd been given a free rein with the script. Not a word had been altered. When she'd started as an advertising clerk with a much less enterprising firm, every flight of fancy she'd embarked upon had been wing-clipped with faint praise or killed with downright scorn. Originality had been frowned upon and tradition had held primal place, but this firm had recognised from the start her flair for the lilting phrase, the catchy slogan, her undoubted gift for seeing a fashion as new as tomorrow and coining the imaginative caption to make people, reading their newspapers, decide this would be the day they'd go to town and shop.

Her first catalogue had been an instant success, and not a flash-in-the pan either, as her second and third proved. Her greatest satisfaction had come in composing the scripts for the fashion shows and if, sometimes, she knew a pang of nostalgia for what in her earlier years she'd dreamed of doing with her life, studying history and teaching and writing about it, she didn't look back wistfully for long.

Her first job, prosaic though she'd found it, had provided financial security during Father's long illness ... and now he was fighting fit again with no trace of the crippling complaint and back in parish work, but not in Britain, in New Zealand, enjoying with his characteristic zest this second chance life had given him.

Rosamond had elected to stay in Southampton with this go-ahead opportunity-giving firm. She loved Hampshire, and its names, so long associated with beauty and history, had been woven by her into this parade. Spring suits were New Forest Green or Pony

Brown, trim yachting outfits were Buckler's Hard, a
delectable dress in wool so fine it could have been geor-
gette, pastel-tinted and edged with a strawlike fringe,
she'd called Cadnam Thatch; a blue-green creation with
an embroidered neckline and cuffs like the edge of a
crenellated wall was Carisbrooke Castle, and the buyers
from the Isle of Wight were delighted with it. The
Chawton evening gown was pure Jane Austen ... the
fashion show proceeded without a hitch that was visi-
ble, though no doubt as always there would have been
moments of panic in the dressing-rooms.

It was amazing how even when one was intent on
speaking lines describing each creation, how aware one
could be of individual members of the audience. Some,
of course, were from rival firms, many were regular
customers well known to her, but Rosamond had been
conscious from the outset of one man, well on in years.
He was interested in the parade, yes, and he looked
every inch a member of the fashion world, except for a
very tanned skin, but time and again she noticed that
his eyes were more often on her face than on the
models. Why? She shut her mind quickly to that. She
wanted no distractions in this hour.

Beyond question Mr Dellabridge was delighted with
the showing. He escorted her personally afterwards,
among the crowd. She would have been less than
human had she not enjoyed the praise, reward for the
long hours of her own time spent on her script.

Finally her chief said, 'There's someone over here
I've left till last because he'd like a little time with you.
He owns a firm like ours in New Zealand. We met first
in Paris years ago. He rang me last night, and I mentioned that our compere for the show had parents living
in Dunedin. He's in the South Island too, but in Christchurch. He said it's two hundred odd miles from there.
Come along.'

His name was Gaspard MacQueen and he looked
rather younger close up, or perhaps it was just the tre-
mendous vitality that seemed to stem from him in broad

shoulders, massive build and height, high cheekbones. Certainly his sartorial elegance fitted in with his calling, but except for that he could have been typed as a rugged Scots Colonial. But Gaspard, as a name, was surely French, so perhaps in his choice of a career the French side had triumphed. Rosamond shook herself free of such wandering thoughts, a habit of hers, and concentrated on uttering things relevant to the world of fashion. Mr Dellabridge moved on to someone else.

This Gaspard MacQueen still had the intent look. He seemed to be searching her features. She had a feeling he'd not heard a word she'd said.

His eyes dropped to the catalogue in her fingers. He tapped her byline: Rosamond L. Briarley. 'Tell me,' he said brusquely, 'is it Rosamond Louise?'

Her brown eyes widened. 'Why, yes, but how could you guess?'

'It wasn't a guess . . . you couldn't be any other than Louise Rosamond's granddaughter. Is she here watching your triumph? For triumph it certainly is. You have all of Louise's gift with words.'

It almost took Rosamond's breath away. But she saw the link.

'Then you knew her in New Zealand? All those years ago?'

'I did. Very well. More than half a lifetime ago.'

A strange feeling smote Rosamond. From her rostrum she'd put him down as tough, rock-hard, but something in his voice, pure nostalgia, she thought, transformed him into something much more vulnerable than rock.

He didn't break into explanatory speech. He seemed single-purposed—sparing of words too. 'Where is she? Far away?'

Rosamond said, 'Very far . . . beyond . . .'

He didn't apologise for breaking in. 'Not——'

She realised he'd thought she meant Gran was dead, beyond recall. 'Oh, not that. I was going to say:

"Beyond these shores." They went to Canada years ago. Grandfather took a professorial post there. Gran did part-time lecturing too, still takes a few lectures at times.'

"In history and English?'

She nodded. He pursed his lips. 'Well, that would certainly be more her line.'

Rosamond wanted to ask: *Than what?* But something kept her silent. What an odd conversation to be having in the midst of this fashion-conscious crowd. However, they were dispersing now. She said, 'I must say goodbye to some of them, but I'd like to come back to you. Would you wait?'

'I'll wait.' As she murmured trifles to those who had lingered, she was conscious that he was waiting with all his might and main. When she got back to him, her chief was with him again. 'Gaspard tells me he knew your grandmother years ago in New Zealand. Pity she's in Canada. She'll be very interested when you write to tell her. Was she in drapery too, Gaspard?'

He shook his leonine head. 'No, she was rather more intellectual than that. She was going to university and specialising.'

A line creased Rosamond's brow. 'But Gran's no blue-stocking snob, never has been. Neither is Grandfather.'

How odd . . . she'd said *is* Grandfather, not *was*. Well, he'd been such a darling, such a kindred spirit to his grandchildren, it was hard, even now, to think of him in the past tense.

Mr Dellabridge said, 'How about coming to our place for an hour or two tonight, Gaspard? And you, Rosamond? Sorry I can't ask you for dinner, but we're going to our son's for that. We'll be home by eight-thirty, though. We're baby-sitting for them while they're at a cocktail party.'

Gaspard MacQueen accepted with alacrity, then said, 'But perhaps that'll rush you, Harry. Miss Briarley, would you have dinner at my hotel instead, and we could chat after it? Or if that's too short a notice, perhaps Monday night?'

'I'm sorry. Tomorrow's my last day at work before I go off on holiday.'

He seemed inordinately disappointed. Liked his own way, Rosamond suspected ... a bulldozer. Then he smiled and it softened his face completely. 'Then that's my loss. I'd like to see as much of you as possible. I must be glad, however, that I didn't miss you entirely. It was like seeing the years roll up like a blind ... I could have imagined I was watching Louise read. Can you make it to Harry's this evening? Good ... I'll pick you up in a taxi if you tell me your address.'

She shook her head. 'I've a Mini, if you don't despise so tiny a car. It looks like rain, anyway, so taxis will be scarce. What hotel?'

Mr Dellabridge moved off and this strange New Zealander said to Rosamond, 'Would you wear exactly what you're wearing now?'

Again she had that puzzling sense of vulnerability in this man. 'I can, but why? It's very plain. I always think the compere must be in a simple, severe style.'

He didn't look in the least embarrassed. 'Sheer sentiment. Your grandmother suited cream. I took her to a Varsity Ball, and no one could hold a candle to her. Sponge-cloth was all the rage. She wore a spray of Seven Sister roses at one shoulder, and a Whitby jet necklace just like you're wearing now.'

Her hand came up to her throat. 'It's a genuine Whitby jet, not the plastic beads that so often pass for it now. But not everyone recognises that.'

He nodded. 'One of my grandmothers came from Whitby. She was brought out to New Zealand as a child in the early days. She left me some of her jet.'

Rosamond was glad to be going out. It had been a frantically busy month preparing for the show and she would have felt very flat when all was over. At times like this she still missed Jeffrey and was annoyed that she did. Odd that he too had been a New Zealander. That country at the bottom of the world seemed to crop up in her life. Not that Gran had ever talked much about the country of her birth. Even when she knew Jeffrey came from there she hadn't asked him much about it. She'd been on holiday here in England during the time of Rosamond's engagement but had found no common ground with Jeffrey in spite of making a real effort to do so. When they had parted Gran had been more bracing than sympathetic; she had said, 'You'll get over it. One does. You may even live to thank your God that Jeffrey wouldn't wait till you saw your father through this bad time. I'd say good riddance. Weep a few tears over him, of course, it gets it out of your system and makes you feel all romantic, but in five or six years you'll hardly remember what he looked like, my girl.'

It was a very pleasant evening. Sybil Dellabridge was so delightfully natural, much loved by her husband's staff, very understanding when they talked shop flat out, and why shouldn't she be, she always said, when Harry had snatched her from behind the counter?

Inevitably, Harry wanted to know all Gaspard's plans for his business and sightseeing trip. He'd been in Britain before but had never managed to see all he wanted to.

Rosamond said, 'What places have priority in your plans, Mr MacQueen?'

He smiled, 'Well, Whitby, naturally, but first I want to see the Isle of Wight. My mother came from there. I aim to hire a car and really explore it. Last time I left it to the last and got called back to New Zealand before I could go.'

Rosamond didn't know what made her offer: 'Mr MacQueen, although I leave for Yorkshire on Tuesday for most of my holiday, I'm spending a long weekend on the Isle of Wight, taking my Mini across from Lymington to Yarmouth, the route I like best. I know it all so well. It belongs very specially to my favourite period of history ... the Stuart reign. But apart from that it's such a darling island, only twenty-two miles by thirteen, but every acre sheer beauty. Would you like to come with me? I'm just staying where the fancy takes me.'

The Dellabridges were delighted for Gaspard. Sybil said, 'It's like one of the real-life coincidences you read about, Rosamond compering the show and Gaspard turning up from thirteen thousand miles away and seeing just a name and an initial on the catalogue. It's not as if she had the same surname as her grandmother's maiden one.'

'She didn't need it,' said Gaspard. 'Louise looked exactly like this. She must have been younger, but she had the same nut-brown hair with golden ends, the same velvety eyes, even the same clear-cut line of chin ... it was almost uncanny. And Rosamond's not a very common name.'

Rosamond said slowly, 'And of course your name is most uncommon. It seems so strange that Gran never mentioned anyone of that name, I'd have remembered it for sure. It's the French equivalent of Jasper, isn't it? Does that mean your mother came from a line of French emigrés, who fled to the Isle of Wight during the Revolution?'

He nodded. 'Gaspard was their surname originally. It became a given name in succeeding generations of the sons of daughters. My grandsons have names that retain the French spelling too, Matthieu and Pierre. Rosamond Louise, this will be a weekend to remember, Louise's daughter taking me to see the scenes my own mother knew and loved. She told us so many stories of the island when she was tucking us down. I want to walk down Shanklin Chine, and up again. Can we manage that? I'll think about my mother as we do it. She talked of thatched roofs in the old village there, and of artists painting the church and cottages at Godshill ... we have one of Haslehust's prints at home, of that ... and the multi-coloured sands of Alum Bay. We have some in a jar on a mantelpiece.'

Rosamond was glad she'd made the offer. She liked

the glimpse of the sentimentalist behind that granite-looking exterior.

She had no idea till that weekend what a delight it was to show someone for the first time, especially someone from Down Under, the glories of that small island so dear to her heart ... the curving bays and headlands, the sheared-off white cliffs gleaming in the sun, the rose-embowered cottages, the enchantment of the trees, the cuckoo calling.

As they went down the magically terraced stone steps of the Chine, so contoured by nature into symmetry and elegance, and shaded by such a delicacy of leaf-tracery and shifting sunlight and shadow, she had the feeling that it wasn't an old man who walked at her side, but an eager child, who'd first seen the greys and blues and greens of the Chine, that deep and entrancing cleft, through the eyes of his imagination as his mother told her stories in the deepening twilight of an Antipodean summer.

In silence they sat on the shore, gazing into an infinity of sea and sky. Then the old man said, 'You've guessed, of course, Rosamond, that I loved Louise with every breath in my body. Loved and desired her with body, soul and mind. It all seemed plain sailing. It was so right, such a promise for a bright future for us both.'

She nodded. 'Yes, I sensed you must have loved her. What went wrong, Mr MacQueen?'

'I allowed someone to make mischief. It seems incredible now, but I'd always wondered that anyone so lovely and with such a mind could have loved me. So my pride was hurt. I felt deeply disillusioned. There's a hard streak in the MacQueens—my grandfather had it, my father had it. It made them successful men. I didn't know I had it till—till that time. But it was there and it carried me through or I'd have gone under out of sheer misery.

'Life goes on, of course. I married, had a son and a daughter. In business I was well on the way to becom-

ing a petty tyrant, too successful by far. Work meant
more to me than anything. It was a challenge, a sort of
pitting my wits against everything . . . against the end of
the Great Depression, the war years, booms, and minor
slumps. Then one day the person who'd made the mischief confessed, and told me the whole truth. At first a
wave of bitterness for all that might have been swamped
me, mentally and physically. But not for long. Knowing
what I then knew gave me back Louise, gave me back
my ideals, my dreams, my untarnished memories of her.
There was nothing to be done, of course. I made en-
quiries, found she had married well, was in her rightful
sphere.

'It saved me from making other mistakes. I could
have ruined my son's life, could have forced him to
follow me in business, instead he lives his life as he
wants to live it. He and his wife are in Canada just now,
and have served their country well through all the years.
There have been many compensations. My two grandsons are splendid fellows. One's in the business with me
full-time, the other pitches in whenever there's an emer-
gency. I'm not as ruthless as once; I'm a better boss—
God, I was hard! And now . . . this has been a bonus,
Rosamond Louise.' He chuckled. 'Isn't it funny . . . I'm
getting the biggest kick of all out of the fact that you,
who could have been my own granddaughter, in drapery, my own trade.

'Tell me, Rosamond, is Louise happy? I won't ask
has she had an easy life, for few lives are easy, and in
any case, Louise was more likely to make it easy for
other people. For herself she'd want a challenge, want
to cope with something. Am I right, tell me? Did she
face up to what life offered, and find happiness in doing
it? In her marriage? I want that for her, Rosamond.'

'That's exactly what she did, Mr MacQueen—faced
life gallantly. I don't think it asked too much of her, if
so, we couldn't have guessed. She's such fun, so ready
always to see the funny side of things. The bouts of
giggles we've shared, Gran, my brother and myself.

And as for Granddad. . . .' She paused, and again
hardly knew why she changed the tense she should have
used. 'Granddad is all you'd have wished him to be as a
husband for your Louise. Bookish, yes, but never too
immersed to take time off for picnics, accompany her to
the orchestral concerts she so loves. He's always wondered what he's done to deserve her.'

She looked up from her contemplation of the sea and
saw that he was moved, but not resentful, just happy.
That night, at a hotel near Freshwater, she tried to analyse why she hadn't told him Gran was a widow. She
came to the conclusion she had been instinctively pro-
tective towards Louise who might not want these memories revived. Louise who'd told her loved grandchild
she might look back in thankfulness that she'd not married her first love. Besides, Gaspard might look on *her*
as his first and true love, but who was to know how
Louise looked upon *him*? There was that strange thing
Gran had said long ago. Strange because she so seldom
talked of New Zealand.

They'd been reading Kipling's *Sussex*, where he had
spoken of the 'one spot beloved over all' and the young
Rosamond had said, 'I know the spot I love most in my
world, Gran . . . Shanklin Chine. You took me there
first on my tenth birthday. What's yours?'

Louise Briarley's velvety brown eyes had looked back
in time. 'Mine is a New Zealand lake with blue-green
waters and snowy mountains reflected in it, and Paradise ducks flying against the sky. A solitary place,
where no roads came or any traffic, only little boats
across the water, and the baaing of sheep upon a
hundred hills.'

Rosamond had been startled at the longing in
Louise's voice and had been aware suddenly of her
grandmother as a person, not just Dad's mother.
She said, 'Why did you ever leave it?'

Gran was never evasive or set back children's curiosity. She said simply, 'I fell in love with someone I
shouldn't have fallen in love with, on a remote sheep

station there. Perhaps I was more in love with the setting, I don't know. But it wasn't to be, and I took up
the Oxford scholarship I'd won, and in time I met your
grandfather, but for sheer beauty, that's remained my
one place beloved over all.'

So the love of *her* life couldn't have been Gaspard
MacQueen, draper. For a moment regret touched Rosamond. How wonderful if this had been the man Gran
had loved and lost all those years ago. Then she, Rosamond, might have played fairy godmother, given him
Louise's Canadian address, told him Louise was once
more free. And that she was still young at heart.

But it wouldn't be fair. It could raise hopes in this
granity-vulnerable man who had unburdened himself to
her. Let sleeping dogs lie, Rosamond. They've lived
their lives. She was just getting carried away by the
romance of it, and this odd feeling of utter kinship with
a man from half a world away, who just might have
been her own grandfather. A tantalising thought, no
more. Forget it.

The next day she was further entranced to find Gaspard
sensitively responsive to not only the beauty surround-
ing Carisbrooke Castle but to the pathos of Charles the
First knowing imprisonment there. She stood with him
gazing out over the wall, sensing in him a need for
silence, as he slipped back three centuries.

Finally he said, 'On such a day as this *he* must have
stood here, gazing south, willing the winds to be as fair
for him when a ship would come in, under cover of
darkness to bear him to France ... and life. Yet it had
to be that other shameful way. When he left here it was
for London and death. And we, as a nation, committed
that foulest of crimes ... regicide.'

A small cry escaped Rosamond. She tried to choke it
back. That intensely spoken 'we as a nation' really got
her. Here was a man, born in the Antipodes, still iden-
tifying himself, in shame, with that dark page of history, centuries old. She wasn't able to check the tear

that fell and splashed on to the dusty golden stone of the parapet. Gaspard looked down on it, then quickly up at her, said, 'Why, lass, I didn't mean to sadden you, grieving over "old, unhappy far-off things," as Wordsworth puts it.'

Rosamond looked up at him with Louise's eyes, said, as she would have done, 'It's not much to shed a tear for him. We should.'

All he said was: 'Aye.'

Presently she said, 'Gaspard,' and saw his eye kindle as she used his name for the first time, 'I find it endearing that you've such a feeling for history. It makes it more of a pity than ever that you and my grandmother didn't marry.'

He said slowly, 'It was because of her that I came to love history. I knew we needed more interests in common if we were to have a good life together. There were others in the field, more of her world. But then the mischief was made and I thought Louise hadn't given me long enough to find common ground. However, it wasn't that at all. You were so right, girl, when you said she wasn't an intellectual snob. But I was touchy. But no matter now. I might have gone all my life disillusioned about Louise. At least the mischief-maker gave me back my belief in her.'

Rosamond said softly, 'And until now you've never been able to talk to anyone about it, because you couldn't hurt your wife.' The pansy-brown eyes met the brilliant blue ones. Rosamond added, 'Because, of course, the mischief-maker wouldn't have been cruel enough to have told your wife.'

The graven lines each side of his mouth deepened with an old pain. His voice was toneless. 'Yes, she knew. *She* was the mischief-maker, Rosamond, and confessed it.'

He saw the angle of her jaw tighten, her lips compress, then she drew in a deep breath. 'I don't quite understand. Might it not have been better if she'd never confessed? How did it come about?'

'Ellie had an accident, a very bad one. She thought she was going to die and suddenly found she couldn't with that on her conscience. So she told me, begged my forgiveness.'

'And you forgave her,' said Rosamond softly.

'Aye. She was a good soul, apart from that one cruel lie. She did love me, according to her lights, but possessively. I've never voiced a criticism of her to anyone before, Rosamond, but to me, you're someone special, almost as if you were Louise's and mine. She was ambitious too, and certainly helped me make a success of the business. She was a good mother to our son ... she "looked well to the ways of her household and ate not the bread of idleness" as the Scripture has it, but ... but she wouldn't have shed a tear for a beheaded king of three centuries ago. We were moderately happy, even after that. What am I saying? We were happier after it, oddly enough, because I lost my bitterness and ruthlessness in business. Meeting you like this, girl, has turned the clock back, and as I've said, I'm no end chuffed to find that despite the academic barrier I falsely believed separated us, Louise's granddaughter is in my own sphere. As if you're the child of my spirit, if not of my flesh.'

She didn't tell him that she too had had academic leanings, but had had to abandon that training when her father was so ill because she needed to earn money immediately. It might take from him this simple joy of finding her in shop life.

They crossed to Lymington again, and took a leisurely way home through the New Forest. They picnicked for lunch in a leafy glade. Rosamond sat back against the bole of a beech tree. She wore the Whitby jet necklace over her fine cream wool sweater. Gaspard's eyes were on it. 'Did your grandmother give you that?'

'Why, yes. Gran believes in sharing out her treasures in her lifetime. She gave some of her jewellery to my Canadian cousins too. Dad's brother lives near her.'

'Treasures, did you say? Did she tell you the story behind that one?'

'Not exactly.'

She could hear her grandmother's voice now. 'So you fancy that, young Rosamond? I think I like a girl of your generation to have a feeling for old-fashioned things.'

Rosamond had said quickly, 'I won't take it if it's something you're sentimental about.'

Louise had laughed. 'Not this. It may have meant something once but not now. It was just from someone I met briefly on holiday and fancied for a few weeks. Incredible! But it's yours.'

Gaspard saw the reflective look in her eyes. 'What did she say, Rosamond?'

She countered quickly, 'Why, did you give it to her?'

'I did. She didn't want to take it because she knew it had belonged to my grandmother. But I was beating the gun and wanted her to have it there and then and wouldn't take it back when we parted. Even though I thought then that she despised me, I still wanted her to have something tangible to remember me by. I thought she looked on me as a clodhopper, out of her world.'

For a moment Rosamond hated Ellie, his wife, who had made the mischief because she wanted him herself. How could any woman do such a thing to a young man ... make him feel his beloved thought he wasn't polished enough for her? No, she wouldn't tell him what Gran had said. To Gran he must have been just one of her admirers ... not that one-and-only who had lived by the shores of an inaccessible lake.

She said lightly, 'Gran just said if I fancied it I was to have it now, that she herself had first worn it when she was my age. She gave it to me for my twenty-first, Gaspard.'

They had dinner at his hotel. Just before the sweets were brought he excused himself and went away up to his room. When he came down he had a box in his hand. He put it on the table, opened it, said, as he showed her a jet bracelet lying on yellowed satin, 'It matches the necklace. I would like you to have it. It would seem very fitting and would please me no end if you'd accept it, Rosamond. I'd like them paired up, would you?'

She hesitated, then seeing the real entreaty in his eyes, and guessing he was re-living a dream because she was so like his lost Louise, she consented.

He said, looking embarrassed for a moment, 'I had a crazy feeling I might be able to look Louise up on this visit, and that I might find I could give it to her. But this will do instead, and when she sees the two together, she might be quite happy to know we'd met.' He cleared his throat. 'Tell me about your father's Dunedin parish. How he likes it, how he likes New Zealand life in general. How your mother likes it.'

'They love it so much they're thinking of settling there permanently, if I join them. I've not quite decided. I've a very good job here and I doubt if Dunedin would have anything comparable. Auckland might, but it's at the top of the other island, and it's pretty costly to visit the Far South often from there, I'm told.'

Gaspard looked at her seriously. 'Christchurch is a large city. MacQueen's is the biggest and the best in department stores there. Our fashion department is fabulous. We could do with someone of your experience and ability ... your flair with words. How about it? Come across and duplicate for us your show here. Only not a springtime parade, an autumn one.'

She blinked. 'Autumn? Oh ... I see.'

He chuckled. 'Autumn is in April in the southern hemisphere, dear child.'

Not only the seasons were turning upside down for Rosamond. This man was taking her breath away. He saw her indecision, pressed his advantage. 'Think it over during the night. I'll ring you before you leave for Yorkshire. Give me your answer then. Think how glad your parents would be. Dellabridge wouldn't be surprised. He said to me he was sure you'd go out to them eventually. Think ... you'd be only six hours away by main road from your people ... you can have a staff car any weekend you like. It's just forty-five minutes by jet plane. You're going to be away two weeks ... add a month to that, and that would give Dellabridge's six weeks' notice. You could just take off from Heathrow.'

She said breathlessly, 'I'll have to think about it. I—I wonder if Mr Dellabridge would just give me six months' leave ... then I wouldn't have burned my bridges behind me. If I didn't like it, I could come back.'

'Fair enough. Don't believe in rushing people.'

She burst out laughing. 'You don't ... Oh, you old fraud! You're just a bulldozer!'

He grinned back. 'My grandson, Matthieu, would be just delighted to have someone take over the advertising. Pierre, now, has a flair for it, but he's in the States for an indefinite period. His wife is having treatment there. But Matthieu would see you nicely settled in.'

She looked apprehensive. 'You mean if I went in six weeks' time you wouldn't be there?'

'No, I've a yen to see Russia this time and I've business in Paris and in Czecho-Slovakia. We have a big department for crystal and glassware, and deal in that country quite considerably. But Matthieu would have a flat ready for you. I could phone him from here. If Pierre hadn't been away, he might have accompanied me. They tried to tell me I was getting a bit old for solo travel!'

Rosamond made up her mind. 'I'll go. No need to ring me in the morning. Oh, how thrilled and excited my parents will be! I'll cable them from Yorkshire. I'll see you in three months' time, then, at the other side of the world.'

Her car was parked near the hotel. He walked to the outer lobby with her. Rosamond had the strangest feeling of unreality. They stood beside a tinkling fountain screened with potted plants. A tiny wrought-iron staircase led up from here. She had the oddest feeling of reluctance to say goodbye, even for three months, to this man who'd been a stranger to her till last Thursday afternoon.

Seemingly he had, also. He put out his hands, took her elbows, drew her a little nearer him. 'Goodbye for now, dearest of girls, and take care of yourself on the roads. Thank you for one of the happiest, most memorable weekends of my whole life.' He smiled, and once more his face was wholly softened. 'You have renewed my youth for me. Goodnight, darling.'

There was only one thing to do. She reached up, took his face between her young, cool fingers, stood on tiptoe and kissed him full on the lips. She knew he wasn't seeing *her*, holding *her*, he was seeing Louise, holding Louise, as she had been half a century ago.

As she stepped back, a movement on the landing above caught her eye. She looked up directly into the face of a man who was wearing the most hostile and disgusted expression she'd ever seen on any stranger's face. Instinctively she recoiled, but recovered instantly, said lightly, 'Goodnight, Gaspard,' and was gone.

Nevertheless, as she drove, she was aware that that brief encounter had tarnished for her the memory of a unique weekend. She'd touched hands with a romance of yesterday, found in an old man a kinship of spirit in appreciation of long-loved island scenes and ancient history, and she hated the fact that someone, even an unknown someone, had thought what that man was thinking.

By the time she'd had a hot bath, had brewed herself some tea, and settled in bed with a whodunnit, she suddenly saw the funny side of it. Perhaps it was rather fine, after all, to meet up with someone who didn't like this permissive age, and who had scowlingly disapproved of a girl in her twenties renewing a man's youth! How ambiguous speech could be. She was glad Gaspard hadn't seen that look, had no idea they'd been overheard. It just didn't, couldn't matter. She was going to a new life, she would never see that man again.

Six weeks later the jet Rosamond had transferred into from Auckland was dropping out of the sky at Christchurch. She had loved every moment of the long flight from London, because Gaspard, away from Southampton when she returned from her holiday, had left every detail meticulously in hand. It had given her three days in Los Angeles, to give her a rest, he had said in his note, and three in Honolulu. She had reached Auckland in a dawn that seemed different from any other because this was the land on which the sun rose first, a brand-new day for the entire world. This seemed symbolic to her.

She had gone through Customs in Auckland, so now, here in Christchurch, she would be meeting Gaspard's grandson in just a matter of minutes. Gaspard's letter had also said that the showroom buyer would be giving her dinner at her home for her first evening, in company with Matthieu MacQueen, and then, as no doubt they'd have a flat for her by then, they would settle her in.

She came through the big doors to hear the loudspeaker system calling her. 'Paging Miss Rosamond Briarley from the U.K. Please call at the International Information Counter, where Mr Matthieu MacQueen is waiting.'

She stopped, asked where this could be found, moved on confidently. She saw an elderly man who couldn't possibly be anyone's grandson, and two women who'd just stopped to speak to a much younger man at the counter. Rosamond caught the tail-end of their conversation, not much more than a greeting, evidently. '. . . .Nice to have seen you again, hadn't realised you were home again—goodbye, Matthieu.'

So this was certainly him. She came up to the side of him, smiling. She didn't have to say, 'Are you Mr MacQueen?' she had her hand half out when he turned. The next moment they were staring at each other with dismayed incredulity.

In fact, on Rosamond's side it was sheer horror. This was the man who had looked down on her from that landing in Gaspard MacQueen's hotel, with such condemnation and loathing.

No wonder ... he'd put the worst possible construction on his grandfather's ambiguous words and had witnessed what must have looked like a lover-like farewell.

Now ... 'My God ... *You!*' he exclaimed.

Rosamond knew she looked the picture of guilt.

CHAPTER TWO

THE hideous moment held Rosamond in a speechless grip. Her mouth had gone dry, she felt she couldn't cope with words till this burning colour had subsided from her cheeks, her throat. It began to ebb and a real weakness succeeded it. With a terrific effort she managed to master that, but still speech would not come. What did one, could one say to explain the ambiguity of those words this man's grandfather had uttered and which, between her and Gaspard, had been something to treasure in memory?

Matthieu MacQueen's voice held a sarcastic note which rasped like a steel file along the edge of Rosamond's nerves. 'I can see this is a bad moment for you, Miss Briarley. Naturally you didn't dream you'd ever meet again the man who overheard that extremely illuminating conversation between you and my grandfather! Neither did I imagine that the dress show compere he raved about was no less than the renewer of his youth on an Isle of Wight weekend. How very unfortunate for you, and how extremely wily of the old man. Oh well, no fool like an old fool, I suppose. And perhaps I should be glad my grandmother is beyond being hurt ... this time.'

That did it . . . *this time*. Rosamond came to life. The brown eyes, velvety no longer, flashed. 'I've no idea what you mean by *this time*. If your grandfather happens to be a philanderer, I can't help it, though I'd find it hard to believe. Has no one ever told you that conversations overheard with no idea whatever of what lies behind them can be most ambiguous? I can explain——'

He held up a hand, but it was the curl of his lip and the utter loathing in the tawny eyes that stopped her. 'Spare me the explanations. With a staff the size of ours, I'm hardly likely to be so gullible I could credit any other meaning than the obvious one. I thought it was rather out of character for my grandfather to consider bringing anyone out from England and more or less creating a position for her, and absolutely laying it on with a trowel in the matter of conditions.

'He not only impressed it on me, when I turned up in Southampton so unexpectedly, that you were to have a really choice flat, but he underlined it in the letter which followed me back to New Zealand. The pantry was to be well stocked, the showroom buyer asked to make you feel at home, one of the firm's cars to be put at your disposal . . . mention of you being allowed off as soon as possible to visit your parents in Dunedin.' A thought struck him. 'Great Caesar! . . . Your father is a minister . . . he said so. I'd never have taken *you* for a daughter of the manse. However, isn't there an old saying that cobblers' wives go barefoot and doctors' wives die young? Well, maybe ministers' daughters are no better than——'

'Be quiet!' she hissed at him. 'Don't finish that sentence. If you do, this entire airport is going to be treated to the spectacle of one of their leading businessmen having his face slapped!'

'Whew! A virago too. Well, well, Grandfather always did like the spirited fillies. We had a very temperamental girl in the showroom once, but he vowed her enthu-

siasms more than made up for the flare-ups. So it all
adds up.'

She was cool again. 'You've never heard of adders-up
who get five from two-and-two? Well, when you finally
realise how far off beam you are, perhaps you'll have
the grace to apologise. If I had a grandfather as fine as
yours I wouldn't believe about him what you're believing. Furthermore, he's a very rugged character. I
shouldn't like to be you if he gets to know about this.'

Still the derisive curl to his lip. 'Oh ... going to go
running to him with the whole sad tale as soon as he
gets back from Europe, are you? I shan't lose any sleep
over that. My grandfather doesn't rule *my* life.'

'I'm certainly not telling any tales, but I can't imagine
anyone as brash and ... and rude as you are not twit-
ting his grandfather with the situation *as you imagine
it*.'

He shrugged. 'It's hardly my business if the old man
likes to make a complete idiot of himself, that is unless
he gets carried away and it looks like affecting the
family. My sister and brother, for instance, and their
families.'

'How on earth could it possibly aff——'

He tapped a foot impatiently. 'Oh, come, don't be so
naïve. I meant money-wise, of course.'

Her eyes widened, then she caught on. She said, 'I
don't wonder some of your employees are temperamental, Mr Matthieu! I've been in contact with you less
than ten minutes and I'm sure I've had so many surges
of blood sugar in that time, I could easily die of a
stroke! Money, except for discussing salary, hasn't been
mentioned between your grandfather and myself. It was
a kindly thought on his part to offer a staff car to go
down to see my parents soon, but I sold my own car in
Southampton, and will buy a secondhand one here as
soon as possible. And, though you probably won't believe it, I'm paying my own fare out. He paid it mean-
time, while I was away on holiday. I feel freer that way.

If I don't like it here ... and judging by the last ten minutes I probably won't, I won't feel bound to stay. My employer in England said come back in six months if I can't settle. The only thing Mr MacQueen paid for, and I couldn't stop him doing that, was to arrange rather luxurious stop-overs for me.' She paused, added, 'I can't, nevertheless, afford what would be a satisfying gesture, and tell you to keep the job. Besides, it would hurt your grandfather, and he's been hurt enough in his lifetime.'

The moment those last words left her lips she wished them unsaid. He seized on them. 'Hurt enough? What do you mean? What hard-luck story has he been telling you?' His hand came up, rumpled his tawny hair in a confused gesture, as he said, 'I hope he's not going off his rocker. You hear of such things ... people have tiny strokes that have no outward sign, but their personality changes ... they forget things, and have delusions. That must be it.'

'It's nothing of the kind. Sometimes it's easier to tell a stranger of some heartbreak, rather than family. And you're so disbelieving I imagine he'd be most reluctant to confide in you. Now, what do we do? Can you take me straight to this flat? After this encounter we don't want to see any more of each other than we have to in business hours.'

'I would love to do just that, Miss Briarley, but our showroom buyer has gone to an immense amount of trouble to give you a dinner in her own home so you feel welcome to New Zealand and I shouldn't like to disappoint her. Neither do I want any hint of—of irregularity on my grandfather's part—to get about. A firm the size of ours can be a hotbed of gossip. For my grandfather's own sake I hope this is a temporary aberration, soon to die a natural death.'

Rosamond couldn't help it. She said in a mock-admiring tone, 'My, my, what big words you use! Then lead me to this shining light among hostesses. And don't worry, I shall be the soul of discretion.'

'I can see you've had lots of practice at it,' he said suavely. 'Your luggage should be through. This way, please.' He sounded exactly like a shopwalker.

Impossible to believe this was the beginning of March. Canterbury was in the grip of one of her famous nor'westers, a hot dry wind that came across the plains after having dropped its moisture content on the Southern Alps, ravaging paddocks and gardens alike with gusts of gale force, and pushing the clouds high so that a clear sky arched over the distant mountains.

It was a bright and beautiful city, laid out with Roman precision on the spreading square miles, and bounded on the south with immense hills of volcanic origin. Eight miles away lay the sea she had seen as they flew in, the Pacific, and south of the hills, she supposed, would be Dunedin and her parents. At the thought her heart lifted a little.

The man beside her wasn't interested in pointing out places of interest to a newcomer, he was too filled with rage and resentment, and it would be a long time before he would be in the mood to listen to her explanation. The discipline that had stood Rosamond in good stead when Jeffrey had first gone away came to her aid and she switched off the tide of dismay that was threatening to overwhelm her.

She said, 'Would you put me in the picture as regards this meeting with the showroom buyer? I appreciate her efforts and it would help to know a little about her. Is she a dedicated career woman?'

'She's a dedicated wife and mother. She worked for the firm in her single days, then when her husband was injured at his work, she came back to us. A series of operations put him right and she says she's had the best of both worlds, a home and a career. She's training in her second-in-command for when she retires. She thinks the world of my grandfather even though she worked for him in his more autocratic days.'

Rosamond said crisply, 'I suppose one needs a bit of steel to get to the top in the rag trade.'

'Perhaps. He drove himself too hard, though, became rather ruthless. Maybe it's the swing of the pendulum now ... softening up in his old age.' The sneer was unmistakable.

Rosamond said, 'I'd rather not discuss your grandfather. We quite evidently see two different people. You've probably been too close to him to see him in true perspective. I saw something very different.'

'On your weekend. On *one* weekend. That entitles you to dismiss what *we* know of him through a lifetime. But I agree, it's *not* for you to discuss him with me.'

She felt her hands clench. They passed a gentle river, the Avon, green-banked and sweet with trees, came into a long road that seemed to lead right to the Cashmere Hills, Colombo Street, but turned to the left and skirted the hills as they reached them, wound round another small river, the Heathcote, pronounced, he told her, as she commented on the name, Hethcutt, then took a steep road up Huntsbury Hill where the Berridges lived.

What glorious gardens, splashed with geraniums as vivid as any in Switzerland, where roses bloomed profusely, and rock-plants tumbled over volcanic rocks set in the undulating ground by the hand of nature, with gardens landscaped round them.

Matthieu MacQueen swung into a drive, went slightly downhill, and stopped the car outside a huge double garage that seemed to cantilever out into space over a gully below, where a tussocky hillside swept down to the plains. They stepped out into a surprising stillness. Rosamond said, 'Why, it's not blowing up here.'

Matthieu said, 'That's a feature of nor'westers. It suddenly, usually in the evening, dies.'

Rosamond was prepared for suave elegance and a cool cordiality, but footsteps were heard running downhill as they turned, and an auburn-haired woman and a teenager, obviously her daughter, almost erupted round the bend of the tree-bordered path.

Thelma Berridge held out both hands, squeezed Rosamond's, said, 'Welcome to this side of the world, my dear, we hope you'll be very happy with us. This is my daughter Barbara, who is in our hairdressing department. Mr Matthieu, John's in his workshop, doing weird and wonderful things with a gadget for the tailoring section. He's dying to explain it to you—makes him feel like Edison or Marconi. That'll give us a chance to get to know Rosamond.'

Some of the alarm and dismay slipped away from Rosamond. Matthieu disappeared and Thelma took her up a path of hill-stones to a terraced lawn, with a view that almost took her breath away. Across the gigantic chequerboard of the pastoral and agricultural plains to the west reared the classical beauty of a vast range of mountains, with that unusual sky of pale green swept clear of cloud by the wind, still busy over there, funnelling up from the cleft valleys where the snow-fed rivers had their sources.

To the east, over the bright patchwork of multicoloured roofs and gardens of the suburbs, lay a sandfringed shore, a glorious place for surfing, Barbara said, but where it ended against the hills of the Peninsula, an estuary where the Avon and the Heathcote met, the waters spread out like rippled pewter among dark pines. The surf-shore curved north in the full sweep of the gigantic Pegasus Bay, that was more like a Bight, till it lost itself beyond the silver-glinting rivers, against more mountains, the Seaward Kaikouras, that ran right down to the sea.

Thelma said, 'And Dunedin is thataway,' swinging her round to face south. 'That green belt beyond the city is Hagley Park and the Main South Road leads through there, and about two hundred and twenty-two miles away is Dunedin. You're to take a long weekend off soon, to see your parents. Either take one of the cars, if you want to see the countryside, or if you want longer at home, you can fly. What's more, your parents are ringing you here at seven-thirty tonight. I've already spoken to them on the phone about it. That was more of Mr MacQueen's arranging. He wrote me at length.'

Rosamond was starry-eyed at the thought, then she was jolted back to apprehension by the knowledge that this would only underline for Gaspard's grandson that she was out to feather her nest and was possibly a threat to the happiness and financial welfare of the family. What made it worse was that she had a niggling suspicion old Gaspard was so carried away by meeting this replica of his true love that he just might want to mention her in his will. If he ever hinted at such a thing, she would have to refuse point-blank.

John and Matthieu appeared. John excused himself from shaking hands because they were oily, but was just as cordial as his wife. 'We love someone new to point out the view to . . . it's a form of selfishness. I feel it has everything . . . fertile plains, mountains, sea-shore, estuary, a lovely city spread out before us . . . nothing more to be desired.'

'Except a lake,' said Matthieu, grinning. 'Horrible of me to point that out . . . and I admit that our lake district lacks the salt sea.'

John grinned, 'He was born in Central Otago, a true Scots background . . . a dyed-in-the-wool Otago-ite.'

Rosamond wasn't interested. 'Tell me, over there . . . around that estuary, are there boating harbours? Is much boating done?'

'Yes, a lot, and at Redcliffs, and over the Port Hills at Lyttelton Harbour with its many bays. Why, are you keen?'

'Yes, I like messing about with boats. I've lived so long in Southampton, and made friends with people who were mad on boats . . . launches, not sail . . . I've been on the water a lot.'

Barbara grinned. 'Oho, you're going to be most popular with the rest of the family. My brothers, Mark and Jerry, have a launch at Charteris Bay on the har-

bour—well, at a small bay near there. We have a weekender of our own. You'll be able to spend weekends
with us. And Rosamond ... I can call you that, can't I?
... I'd love to set your hair for you this weekend. What
say I pick you up tomorrow evening at your flat and
bring you round here and style it for you? I've all the
gadgets. You'll want to make a good impression on the
staff on Monday ... they're expecting something ... a
dream-show compere brought all the way from the
U.K. So, even if you've met the big boss already, I'm
sure——'

Matthieu cut in. 'Maybe you feel as a hairdresser,
Babs, that you can certainly improve on nature, but I
must assure you no one could have made a bigger impression on me than Miss Briarley did at our very first
meeting, hair-do or not.'

His eye flickered in Rosamond's direction and he
laughed, and only she knew the innuendo behind the
apparently complimentary words.

Rosamond kept her colour down and laughed too
and said, 'Thank you, Barbara—at the end of a fairly
long flight, anyone would be glad of some grooming. I
was too intent on seeing all there was to be seen in
Hawaii to hunt for a hairdresser. I feel overwhelmed
with all this kindness ... I insisted on paying my own
fare out, but with Gaspard arranging the lovely stop-
overs, and this promise of a weekend to see my parents,
I feel as if I've suddenly acquired a fairy godfather.' She
looked straight at Matthieu. She'd used his grandfather's given name deliberately. Any over-formality
and this man would call it hypocrisy. He'd heard her
call his grandfather Gaspard in Southampton.

Thelma nodded. 'That's just what he was to us when
John's health caused us concern for a few years. I
proved myself first, I know. I worked very hard to bring
the showroom up to top sales, but I came to feel secure
and hopeful because of Matthieu's grandfather. So I
imagine this wasn't just an impulsive gesture on his
part, he must have been really impressed with your

ability. He wrote me in some detail about it. I'm tremendously thrilled we can stage an autumn showing early next month, if you can run it on the same sort of lines as the spring one in Southampton. Gaspard mentioned your choice of local names for the models. Do you think you could contrive something as individual for us?'

They couldn't miss the light of inspiration that flashed into the brown eyes. Rosamond waved a hand that took in hills and mountains, sea and shore, said, 'This is already happening. As a matter of fact I dashed up to London to New Zealand House before I left, and got all the brochures I could on Christchurch—and of the whole of Canterbury—and I worked some out on the long haul here, thousands of feet above the clouds. This is an inspiring setting. I'll need to get some extra local information from you, though, Mrs Berridge.'

It was a comfortable type family home, well kept without being over-tidy, with endearing evidences of the children's hobbies scattered about, and books everywhere. Had it not been for Matthieu and his distrust and dislike of her, Rosamond could have been supremely happy on this her first day within the New Zealand shores.

Just as dinner was ready, the boys came in, in disreputable jeans, each carrying a string of fish. Mark was a little older than Barbara, Jerry younger and a seventh-former. He was naïvely outspoken. 'Say, you're really something, Miss Briarley! I'd had an idea that having reached the top with fashion shows you'd be almost in the sere and yellow, you know ... very sophisticated and made up to hide the wrinkles, but tough. But you don't look much older than some of Mark's girl-friends, so I don't have to be scared of you. I tried to dodge being home tonight, but Mum wasn't having any of that. And Babs has just told me you like messing about with boats. That's neat. How about coming out with us next weekend?'

They all chuckled at his nerve, but Matthieu said,

'Poor show, Jerry, but my ancient grandfather stonkered that. He's just as bowled over as you, and he's jacked it up with your mother that she's to take off to see her parents in Dunedin next weekend.'

Rosamond didn't look at him. He wasn't missing any chances of gettings digs in. She turned to John Berridge. 'It's wonderful to my mother and myself that Dad is in full health and strength after years in a wheelchair. Surgery and treatment did wonders for him. You'll realise what it means to him, seeing you had a similar experience. It's been worth everything we had to do to have him in parish work again.'

John nodded. 'It went against the grain with me at first, to see Thelma having to work so hard, disguising from me that she hated not being home when the children came from school, but she made it to the top, and now, somehow or other, we wouldn't have been without that experience. We enjoy everything we can do together now, all the more because once we couldn't.'

Rosamond nodded. 'It works that way. At first, with us, it turned everything upside down. I just couldn't go on studying. I wasn't far enough through, and simply had to be earning, and hadn't trained for anything else. My brother had just taken on a big engineering job in Canada, a marvellous chance for him. There was nothing comparable that he could get in England, so he had to take it, but always helped with money. Greg's a grand chap. I had a knack with words so I became an advertising clerk. Between Greg's money and mine, it meant Mother could stay home to look after Dad.'

Thelma looked at her shrewdly. 'And at first you'd hate it, then you'd find, to your surprise, that you were enjoying it.'

'Yes, but how did you guess?'

'The way your eyes lit up when you spoke about the inspiration the Canterbury scenery was going to be to you for our show.'

Rosamond caught a fleeting look of surprise on Matthieu's face. She could have laughed ... he values

Thelma's opinion and it's taken him aback to think that I'm good at my job, that it isn't just for personal reasons his grandfather brought me here, she thought.

'I did hate it at first. It was stupid, but I had to switch from writing poetry and essays what-have-you, using words in their finest sense, to use them to describe merchandise in which I was scarcely interested at all. I was horribly snooty about it, inwardly. Then—well, I suddenly got over it.'

Thelma looked at her. 'Anything specific change you? Or do you mean you suddenly became aware you were enjoying it?'

Rosamond's eyes went reflective. 'I can pinpoint it. I'd done an ad about clothes for special occasions, how they can subtly change one, not just in looks but in confidence. I happened to be in the showroom when this woman came in, who had the clipping of the ad in her hand, so I lingered near. She got a very nice girl on the staff to serve her, someone genuinely interested in people. The woman confided in her, "I'm to be the mother of the bridegroom at a very fashionable wedding and I'm out of my element. I've a flower farm in Cornwall and out in all weathers. Not much time to titivate myself, look after my hands, my hair." Then she told us they'd managed to put their son through medical school and he was marrying a gorgeous girl but her people were socially above them, though "They don't patronise us, so for their sake, and my son's, I'd like to do them proud on the big day, and this ad made me feel I could. Would you help me?"

'We did enjoy ourselves! We kitted her out from foundation garments out, got our beauty counter to work wonders with make-up that didn't take anything away from her personality, and the way she blossomed was like a performance of *My Fair Lady*. She was sweet, gave us a lovely coloured photo of the wedding, and some wedding-cake. From that moment I stopped resenting my change of training. I was still dealing with people, but with their material needs instead of the minds of students, whom I'd hoped to teach, eventually.'

John nodded. 'Yes, I found out that too ... that liking what you do is far more important than doing what you like.' He chuckled. 'How I despised the basket-making and carving which was all I could do for a bit! I'd always worked with steel, in big industry. Some more mutton, Rosamond?'

'No, thank you, that was delicious, especially with those broad beans with the tangy sauce ... was it lemon juice in white sauce? It was. But that tamarillo trifle looks so tempting, I'm leaving space for it. They look like a cross between blackberry and mulberry.'

Barbara glowed. 'I made that. We used to call tamarillos tree-tomatoes, but they're a citrus fruit, egg-shaped and sized, and strangers thought because of their name that they must be savoury. Sales pepped up immediately they changed the name. You just cut them in half lengthwise, stew them very gently with sugar, slip the skins off, pulp them, and put them over sponge and pour the custard on. So easy.'

Despite all the kindness, and the feeling of kinship with this family, the long air journey began to tell on Rosamond, but the phone call from her parents revived her. They were using two phones so they wouldn't miss a word.

They assumed that everything about this new position was beyond belief. 'Imagine,' said her mother, 'your new boss arranging luxury stop-overs for you so you're not too fatigued. And the buyer who's entertaining you sounds such a darling. And we'll see you soon. By the way, guess what? We've had a letter from Greg and he's been put on the short list as a technical adviser in certain engineering projects in this country. Something to do with hydro-electrical schemes. Wonderful, if he got it.'

The entire company, with the exception of Matthieu, she supposed, shared her pleasure in this bit of news. Thelma noticed her colour suddenly ebb. She leaned forward, put her hand on Rosamond's as it lay on her lap, said, 'My dear, I think jet-lag has caught up with you. We've enjoyed having you, but we're being selfish. Matthieu and I will take you to your flat now. You'll be glad to get to what you'll soon regard as your own home. Everyone relaxes more in their very own place. Oh, bother, don't tell me we're about to have visitors!'

They were, and some the Berridges hadn't seen for years, so Thelma said, 'Never mind, Matthieu knows where everything is. He'll see you installed. No, Babs, you'll stay talking till all hours if I let you go. So would I, for that matter, and I don't think Matthieu would stay as long.'

As they drove away Rosamond said, 'That's for sure, anyway.'

He said stiffly, 'What's for sure? You've lost me.'

'Thelma's remark before the goodbyes were said. That you wouldn't stay as long as she would, Mr MacQueen.'

'Yes, it's for sure. I've certainly no desire to linger.'

'That makes for two of us.' She sighed and added, 'It's hard to believe you're Gaspard MacQueen's grandson. He's so kindly, so tolerant.'

His laugh was unpleasant. 'That's not always been his reputation.'

She said fiercely, 'And he's the first to admit that, but it's been otherwise for many years now.'

'What do you mean? How could *you* know my grandfather mellowed a lot?'

'He told me ... and anyway, you referred to it yourself.'

'He told you? When? I mean how did it arise?'

She said deliberately, 'He told me that weekend we spent on the Isle of Wight. We paused on the walk round the wall of Carisbrooke Castle where Charles the First must so often have stood, and he told me then.'

'Told you what?' He sounded intensely irritated.

'Told me he'd been well on the way to becoming a tyrant in the world of business. That he'd looked on pitting his wits against the struggle to the top as so much compensation. Then everything changed for him.'

His silence held astonishment, unbelief. Then, 'Good heavens, I'd looked on my grandfather as very reticent . . . with strangers.'

Her voice was cool. 'Perhaps you have it wrong. He could be reticent with his own flesh and blood, but not with strangers. I didn't find him that way at all. We established an instant rapport.'

His voice, in turn, was dry. 'I notice you're good at that. The whole five Berridges fell for you in a big way.'

'That sounds insulting, Mr MacQueen . . . intentionally so. As if I'm all things to all people. It was perfectly natural. They're appreciative of their surroundings, their view. I shared their enthusiasm. The boys are used to handling boats, so am I, and John Berridge has experienced much the sort of crisis in his life that my father did. Naturally we clicked.'

He did not answer her, and she knew a small satisfaction.

Then, 'Your flat is in Park Terrace. They're older Colonial houses there, built by the rich of the day. It's impossible to manage now without domestic help. So many have been divided, quite charmingly, into flats. Nothing but the best for you, Grandfather said. It goes with the job.'

Rosamond felt dismayed. 'Mr MacQueen, I'll take it for a start as I need my own rooftree immediately. But as I've no intention of taking any more than any other employee does, in a little while I shall be looking for my own accommodation at a price I can pay. This is ridiculous, though it was nothing but kindness on your grandfather's part.'

'That sounds admirably independent, but it's nothing to do with me. It's entirely between you and Grandfather. He said it wasn't to be too far from his house. It's within walking distance.'

The inference was insulting and was meant to be. It was no use protesting her innocence to this unbelieving hunk of male. He'd inherited that granite from his grandfather, she suspected, without any of the old man's saving grace. Gaspard had said all the MacQueen men had a hard streak in them.

She didn't think it was any use telling Matthieu that anything Gaspard did for her, he was doing for her own grandmother, for the long-ago lost love of his youth. In any case, Gaspard might not want that known to his grandson. And especially would he want kept secret the fact that Matthieu's grandmother—whose blood ran in his veins—had been capable of such treachery.

They wound round the banks of the Avon and came to a wide street bordered on one side by the river, on the other with large, mostly wooden houses, opulent and gracious.

'It's a front flat, a ground floor one, with quite a choice garden in front kept by a gardener, unless you have a flair in that direction.' Matthieu's tone, she felt, doubted anything so wholesome.

'I have,' she informed him. 'We always had manses with gardens. I'll soon pick up the opposite season technique.'

He fitted the key in the lock, went ahead of her, turned on the lights. It was delightful and far beyond her means, she knew, even if Gaspard had offered her a very generous salary.

The furniture must have been retained from the day when this had belonged to wealthy people. The lounge was all in greys and blues and hydrangea purples and pinks, with elegant tables and lampshades scattered through. An exquisite corner cabinet held choice china, and a davenport fair invited one to write letters. Off it was an alcove study, equipped with a sensibly sized work-desk, stationery, notebooks, fashion magazines, a swivel chair, some filing cabinets. They were obviously new, bought with her needs in mind. The kitchen was the last word in labour-saving devices and charm of decor. There were two bedrooms, a single and a double.

Rosamond put her bag down on the single bed, removed her cinnamon travelling coat and hung it in that wardrobe.

'In *this* room?' Matthieu asked, and she was sure his tone held surprise.

'Yes, of course. The other will be a spare. Between Sundays, on a more quiet week, perhaps, if ever there's such a thing in manse life, my parents will spend time here. I'm not likely to want to make a double bed every morning, when there's a single one.'

She told herself not to be so sensitive. He might not have meant anything. He was most punctilious, showed her a jar full of milk tokens, for the days to come, opened well-stocked cupboards, the refrigerator, pointed out that the small deep-freeze unit above it was stocked with interesting-looking packages.

'Those were not provided by the firm. The Berridges enjoyed filling that. The frozen vegetables and berries are from their own store, and home-grown. They also filled your cake-tins. I'll bring your luggage in now.'

'I'll bring some.' He did not demur. He said, as she went to lift one, 'Leave that to me, it's a ton weight. Oh, well, one doesn't expect a fashion expert to travel light.'

'No,' she said drily, 'it's full of catalogues and brochures . . . they weigh more heavily than mere clothes. How fortunate that Mrs Berridge doesn't mind that your autumn showing is a little later than usual. She says that in Christchurch summer lingers on and that though it's traditional to have an early showing, she's glad of an opportunity to have it later this year . . . she's always thought buying would be keener if the show came after March the seventh when evidently the big income tax payment of the year is made here. That it takes a nip in the air to make people discard their lighter clothing and begin to think about woollen suits and fur edgings.

'Nevertheless, I'm going to have to work hard and fast. Mrs Berridge said that when I go down to see my people first, I could make it a long weekend, having Monday off, but I won't be doing that, I couldn't spare

the time. Shops aren't open on Saturdays here, so I'll
take a late flight Friday and come back Sunday night.'

She asked him to leave the cases in the lounge. 'More
room for unpacking. Then you can go. I won't offer
you anything despite that well-stocked larder, Mr
MacQueen. We agreed that for sure you wouldn't want
to linger. If I turn hospitable you'll be justified in thinking I'm trying to create a more favourable impression.'

'Fair enough.' He was quite uncaring. 'Goodnight,
Miss Briarley. I'll pick you up at twenty to nine
Monday morning. By night you should have this staff
car my grandfather specified.'

'No, don't call for me. I took particular notice on the
way in that I'm not far from the centre of the city. I'll
be exploring tomorrow and will familiarise myself with
the most direct route to the store. And I won't be
having the staff car, thank you. That could cause talk
and jealousy among the staff. I like to be just one of the
herd, with no special privileges. I also like my independ-
ence. Till now I've always had it, and only an old man's
generosity and sentiment has placed me in this position.
Goodnight, Mr MacQueen.'

She felt she had had a very satisfying last word but,
his hand on the door-handle, Matthieu turned, his
mouth twitched in a way she resented and he said, 'You
know, a speech like that is far more likely to create a
good impression than if you *had* offered me some hospitality. You're really very clever, and you have an
undoubted gift with words . . . not only in catalogues!'
and he was gone, leaving Rosamond gritting her teeth.

CHAPTER THREE

ROSAMOND slept the clock round, exhausted not so
much by the air travel as by the devastating meeting

with Gaspard's grandson. He must have turned up in Southampton unexpectedly—had the old man known he was coming, he would have told her, suggested a meeting with him, as one of the management. In fact, he would probably not have gone across to the Isle of Wight then had he known he was coming. It had been unfortunate timing.

Once she had showered and had breakfast she felt a giant refreshed, and couldn't help revelling in the luxuriousness of the setting. The sound of cathedral bells made her whisk round to make her bed, put away some things she'd not bothered to unpack the night before, and decide to go to a service. There was no time to enquire where the nearest Presbyterian church was, but she'd been brought up to be ecumenically minded and in a city like this with a definite centre to it, most roads led to Cathedral Square.

How beautiful it was! She learned later that the spire was a miniature replica of Salisbury Cathedral's. How magnificent of pioneers, living in makeshift homes and on windswept plains, to have a dream already in their hearts that an edifice of worship as beautiful as this should rise some day. So said the brochure she picked up in the vestibule. The singing was harmonious, the atmosphere all she could have wished, the sermon short and compelling. Her nerves stopped jangling. It was stupid even to feel so, but to come so far, so happily, and to meet with such enmity and misunderstanding from the acting head of the firm had half paralysed her. All would be well when Gaspard came back in a few weeks' time. Matthieu would come to realise that the old man merely looked on her as someone two generations removed who had been kind enough to take an old draper from New Zealand to see where his mother had lived.

She spent the entire afternoon working on the ideas she'd jotted down on the plane, from the brochures she had had from New Zealand House, and her first tentative phrases had been quite apt. Some of the booklets

had shown the autumn russets and golds of Canterbury,
fortunately, because from her parents' letters, as they
had naturally written of the differences rather than the
similarities, she had thought of all the trees here as evergreen.

The New Zealand climate had been so kind to the
saplings the pioneers had brought with them, and they
had adapted admirably to a change of season, so that
the magnificent trees of Hagley Park, so near to her
flat, looked as if they'd stood for hundreds of years,
instead of just over one century.

She wrote down 'Avon green teamed with oak scarlet,' and 'Cashmere tussock gold,' remembering the tus-
socks on the lower slopes beneath the Berridge home.
'Cathedral elegance' could be worked in . . . ideas swam
into her mind, stimulated by new scenes. She typed
them on her portable, stowed them in a folder, felt
ready to meet the new job.

However, she still had butterflies in her stomach as
she walked along the riverbank next morning, checking
her directions by the names of the streets that ran from
the banks, and were named after English bishoprics . . .
Gloucester . . . Worcester . . . Hereford and so on.

The architecture of MacQueen's had an elegant soli-
darity with Ionic pillars at the main entrance and some
of the facings were of the exquisitely mottled Takaka
marble. Rosamond had examined the windows when
out walking yesterday afternoon and had seen that the
merchandise ranged from the exclusive to the everyday
utility lines, catering for a wide section of the public.
Thelma was waiting, smiling, at the staff entrance.

'I expect you feel a little nervous, one always does on
a first day till routine establishes itself and things
become known and familiar. It would have been nicer
for you had Mr MacQueen senior been here, seeing
he'd engaged you.'

How true, thought Rosamond hollowly.

Thelma went on: 'Pity you'd not met Mr Matthieu

when he was over there ... I think he said he'd just
missed you, that you'd gone on holiday.'

'Yes, I started my holiday by taking Mr MacQueen
round the Isle of Wight, then went up to Yorkshire to
some cousins. The night of the fashion show I was invited by my boss to his place so I could chat with Mr
MacQueen about New Zealand where my parents were.
When I knew his mother had come from the Isle of
Wight, I offered to take him with me in my car. The job
offer all sprang from that.'

She didn't think Thelma was likely to discuss this
with Matthieu, but in case it ever cropped up, it would
be good for him to know she'd made no secret of that
weekend. Other staff members joined them, were made
known to Rosamond. She was relieved to find she
wouldn't be facing resentment because a new position
had been created, which virtually placed her in the top
position in the advertising section, because the head of
the department was getting married at Easter and as her
fiancé was a farmer away up in North Canterbury, she
couldn't keep her job on.

Monica seemed a happy-go-lucky person, ready to
show Rosamond all the files, chat over the differences
she was likely to find.

'Easter, of course, is a great time for weddings, and
it's late this year, well on in April. But whereas in Britain guests would appear in new spring suits, it's
autumn ones here. But being already over your autumn
in Britain, you'll know the new trends, and also what
took and what didn't. It gives you a head start.'

She was thrilled with the ideas Rosamond had
already sketched out. 'I can see a new country has
already had an impact on you. By the way, I've jacked
up a radio interview for you. Not till Thursday, though.
It gives you time to sort things out. I think it's shocking
when people are asked for their impressions of the
country when all they've managed to see is the interior
of an airport, and their journey to a hotel. It's not a

commercial thing, more on the lines of the fact that we
suffer from too much brain-drain to other countries,
but here's someone in the rag trade actually bringing
her expertise here.'

Rosamond laughed. 'How boosting to one's ego! I
have a Lawks-a-mussy-can-this-be-I feeling. I started on
the bottom rung of the advertising ladder, you know,
but this could be fun. A new experience.'

Monica Payne said, 'You'll do us. We were afraid of
getting somone patronising. It would have been a pity,
because this has always been a harmonious department.
Pity Mr Pierre's not here. He's a wizard at advertising.
But he's in Boston just now.'

Rosamond said, 'These MacQueens do get around,
don't they? I know Mr Pierre's there because of his
wife's operation, but Mr Matthieu seemed to think
nothing of hopping across the world to see his grandfather very briefly.'

Monica nodded. 'I'm not breaking any confidences
about this because it was common knowledge at the
time. Someone here in a very good position was found
out in gross dishonesty. It was quite horrible. If there
was to be prosecution it had to be decided at once, so
Matthieu flew off to consult old Gaspard. It was very
upsetting. The man concerned is excellent at his job and
had been with the firm for many years. Between Gaspard and Matthieu they've got a company in Well-
ington to give him a chance in a position where he
couldn't defraud. He's demoted, of course. His was a
position of responsibility which always carries a higher
salary. But it gave Mr Matthieu a hell of a time before
and after his trip. Not a moment of pleasure in all that
travelling.'

Rosamond felt regret wash over her. Matthieu
MacQueen must have arrived in England feeling very
disillusioned about a long-time employee. He'd found
his grandfather, as he thought, philandering with
someone in her mid-twenties and he'd thought it must
be someone on the make. Then he'd flown back to a

tense situation, possibly to a backlog of other work, then had come face-to-face with a reminder of an episode he'd deemed no more than a passing folly on the part of his grandfather, and had dreaded it might deepen into something that could affect the whole family. She must make allowances for him.

She saw him only twice that week. No doubt he had responsibilities in every department. She was only one cog in the wheel, but his curt manner when he had to deal with her made her wonder if he was trying to impress upon her that she wasn't to expect from him the ridiculous amount of personal interest his grandfather had shown in her.

She had a wonderful weekend with her parents, who were still wide-eyed with the chance out of the blue that had come to her. Carrie Briarley said, 'It's like a fairytale, that Christchurch draper seeing you compere that show and offering you a job here. I hated having you thirteen thousand miles away.'

Rosamond didn't know why she didn't say, 'But it was mainly because my name is Rosamond Louise and he loved Dad's mother long ago.' She was glad she hadn't mentioned it when her father said, 'What do you think? Mother's coming out here for a long holiday this year. I've told her to wait till the New Zealand spring and stay on through the summer. She'll be keener than ever once she knows you're here. We had a feeling this might fall through, so we didn't mention it.'

Rosamond wondered what her grandmother would say when her parents wrote to say she was working in Christchurch for a firm called MacQueen's. She didn't think Gaspard was the love of Louise's life. That man had been a farmer, obviously.

The Sunday night plane she was to take back got grounded for some mechanical fault, and she had to ring Thelma to ask her to let Matthieu know she wouldn't be in till about one on Monday. She preferred that to ringing him direct. Thelma thought nothing about it. 'Oh, well, you know the tag: "If you've time to spare, go by air!" It's always happening. Just enjoy the extra time with your people.'

When Rosamond walked in, Matthieu was in the advertising office going over something with Monica Payne. She came in unheard, paused in the doorway, and heard Matthieu say, 'These are excellent, Monica. I'm not the judge Pierre is, of course, but these have a flash of sheer inspiration about them. I know how Pierre felt about you leaving us, he said that you being a writer instead of only an advertising clerk gave your work an extra fillip, and he wished you were marrying a city chap so we could have retained you, but it looks as if Grandfather made the right decision after all.'

Monica said, 'What do you mean, Mr Matthieu . . . after all? Had you had doubts?'

He grinned, in a way he'd never grinned at Rosamond, and said, 'I thought the old boy—with all due respect to him—had fallen for a pretty face . . . but I'm quite happy to be proved wrong . . . for the sake of the firm, of course.'

'Of course,' said another voice, drily, from behind them. Rosamond's voice.

The two on the desk stools swung round as one. Rosamond added, 'I must be the exception to the rule that eavesdroppers hear no good of themselves. Glad you find me satisfactory, Mr Matthieu. It's taken a load off my mind. I knew you had doubts, of course.'

Monica looked dismayed. What a line to take with a new boss—and in front of another employee! She said, 'I'm due to meet my fiancé for lunch. He's not often in town and I want him to help me choose curtains. Would you excuse me, Mr Matthieu?'

He nodded. 'I expect you find your dinner-hour all too short. How would you like the afternoon off?'

'Oh, how marvellous! I told him he just might have to try to get in again next week, but he's pretty busy just now.'

Matthieu nodded. 'He'll be crutching before he puts

the rams out, I suppose. And ploughing for the winter wheat?'

Rosamond felt mildly surprised. She hadn't expected a draper to be knowledgeable about farming, though with New Zealand so dependent upon primary products, perhaps many were interested in the year's cycle of the sheep farmer. Matthieu added: 'And if you get some of your stuff here, don't get the dockets through till I see them. I'd like you to have a special staff discount.'

Monica sparkled. 'Of course I'm getting them here. I've got them picked out, but I just want Ron's okay.' She disappeared.

Matthieu said, 'Sit down, Miss Briarley. I've a couple of hours free. I thought you might feel less inhibited with Monica out of the way.'

She said cautiously, 'There's been no hint of any resentment, on the part of the staff, that is.'

His lips tightened. 'I get the message. But *my* resentment was entirely personal.'

She felt ashamed of herself. 'I'm sorry, that was uncalled-for. Actually, I've been pleasantly surprised. It would be only natural if some of the staff here had resented me, might have thought one of them could have been promoted, but they've been sweet, and I heard that you'd had a very stressful time just before you flew to Britain. So I can understand——'

He interrupted her. 'Then that's fine. Let's get on from there. Disharmony doesn't make for wheels turning smoothly. We can forget my first impression and simply work together. Now, which of these two models do you think should take precedence?'

They worked on steadily with surprisingly few interruptions. Twice when Rosamond paused for a word Matthieu put it in very aptly. She said, 'Then you're both good with advertising.'

He blinked. 'Both? Who do you mean?'

'I was told your brother had a flair for advertising, but it seems you have too.'

He seemed rather naïvely surprised and pleased. 'I'm used to Pierre being thought of in that line. I don't think it comes naturally to me.'

'Doesn't it? I fumbled twice for words and you came up spot on with the right adjective. That's what advertising is all about, mainly. And even what you rejected half an hour ago showed discrimination. That's part of it too.' She stopped, slightly embarrassed. 'This is rather patronising. I got carried away. After all, you're my boss. Sorry.'

To her surprise he didn't set her back. 'On the contrary, I liked it. I'm not really the boss type. I just put on a big act when I feel a situation needs it. This atmosphere suits my big brother. Yet when I get stuck into it, I come to terms with it.'

Suddenly Rosamond felt that here was a man out of his setting. There was a ruggedness about him that didn't belong to this highly competitive world of exotic perfumes, fabulous fabrics, filmy negligees, ribbons and laces ... he had a skin almost as tawny as his eyes and hair and only his silver-grey impeccably cut suit toned him down. He looked more the outdoor type.

She said, with fellow-feeling, 'It's odd, isn't it, how one does. I could see nothing but teaching or lecturing with a bit of freelance writing on the side, but economic circumstances forced me to abandon my training and I was the most surprised person when I actually found I could enjoy what I was doing. Not perhaps with my whole heart, but enjoy it just the same.'

He nodded, 'Yes, I know it's good to be able to do what's called one's own thing. Sure, I'd have liked to spend all of my life outdoors, but I can't help enjoying this too. In our family's pioneer history two brothers came out here, one to start this business ... a counter of women's clothing, a counter of men's. One went far south, farming. We're a mixed lot. Some of the descendants liked the business ... some liked the farming. Miss Briarley, it's time I made my rounds. It keeps everyone on their toes—not spying, you understand, but keeping them up to scratch. Quite apart from that, it makes the boss available to everyone. Not every young junior has the nerve to tap at the buying-room door and ask to speak to the boss. Some of them have great potential and this is the only way I can assess it in the junior staff. How about walking round with me?' he added. 'Give you more a view of the shop as a whole, rather than individual items being singled out for advertising. I always think the advertising section tends to be somewhat isolated.'

Against her will Rosamond found herself admiring Matthieu MacQueen's attitude towards his staff. He seemed to know most of them by name and where he didn't, he asked. Only one or two looked guilty or nervous when they saw the boss coming into their department, then only when they had been gossiping among themselves instead of approaching customers.

Once Matthieu gestured for her to stop. They were screened from this assistant's view by a pyramid of fancy soaps. The girl was serving at a glass counter. Rosamond stiffened lest this was eavesdropping on something that would earn a reprimand. She wished herself miles away. Then she noticed Matthieu had a half-smile on his lips. The customer decided on some shampoo. The girl said, 'There's a hair-conditioner in that particular brand. Have you tried it? It's not cheap initially, but extremely economical. I use it myself.' That was testimony in itself, she had dark brown hair, shoulder-length, and it swung in a glistening bell. The customer took some. Then the girl picked up a small sachet. 'Lovely for among your handkerchiefs. These are samples.' She offered small talk about the weather, then said, 'We're having a special fashion parade this autumn. We have someone out from Southampton who's really something. Watch the papers for the announcement.' Her parcel was deftly wrapped and handed over.

Matthieu said in a low voice, 'That was what I hoped for. That girl brought that department up from a very

mediocre standard to treble its takings last year, simply
by those sort of tactics. I've heard Grandfather say that
was how the business survived in the Depression, training girls to induce customers to buy more than they
meant to. She's never too pushing and the customers just
love her. She trains her staff in the same procedure. Not
acting only for her own credit either, as you'd realise
... she passed on news of another department. Sheer
enthusiasm is catching, and she loves people. That's the
secret of success in serving the public.'

Rosamond nodded. 'If it starts at the top it works
down, I know. On the lines of if the captain's happy,
the whole ship is.'

He nodded. 'Grandfather is a shining example of this.
He's a tough old boy in many ways, but I think the
whole staff would admit he works as hard if not harder
than any of them. A real goer for his age.'

'Yes, he's positively magnetic. His vigour is not only
amazing, it's also attractive, even infectious.'

He looked at her a little sharply and she added
quickly, 'He nearly walked me off my feet on the Isle of
Wight ... all round the great wall of Carisbrooke,
down Shanklin Chine, then up again, and all the other
chines. We walked far along the shore at Alum Bay,
and every time we got to a bit of accessible beach, he'd
get me to stop the car and we'd scramble round the
rocks. The only thing we missed was seeing Osborne
House, I felt it would be a pity to rush that. I advised
him to go back for that. I hope he did.'

They came to the Manchester Department which was
terrifically busy. Customers were waiting. She expected
Matthieu to move on, come back later for a chat with
the head, but not so. He moved swiftly behind the
counter, approached a young woman wanting flan-
nelette sheeting for making into cot sheets, showed several nursery designs, advised on quality, and as deftly as
any of the others cut it off, asked if she'd liked him to
cut all the lengths for her, saying, 'Our shears are pos-

sibly sharper than yours, and besides saving you time, it's easier on a counter,' followed the procedure he'd admired in the other department by asking if she had enough cotton to stitch them with and made an extremely neat parcel. Finally he put it through the docket book of the most junior counter member, rang it up, gave the change, and rejoined Rosamond.

The glass and crystal department enchanted her most. 'Though I'd be terrified to work here. Imagine showing a customer that Venetian glass! I'd drop it out of sheer fright. Look at that lovely ruby-red goblet. Isn't it exquisite?'

Matthieu handled it nonchalantly himself, turning it this way and that to catch the light. He replaced it, and was turning away with her when a couple of women came up to him, obviously mother and daughter and both ravishing redheads, though Rosamond guessed the older woman owed the brightness to Barbara's department more than to Nature. The girl said, 'Why, Matthieu, I thought you'd have gone back long ago. You've not been over to see us.'

He said, 'Oh, Grandfather's still overseas. I had a quick flip over myself, and I've had my nose to the grindstone since coming back. I'll give you a ring when things settle down.'

The older woman said, 'There's tonight. You're actually having a night at home, aren't you, Verna? Any chance you could come over, Matthieu?'

Rosamond had turned away and was examining some Noritake china called Spring Meadow. She heard him say crisply, 'Sorry, can't be done, unfortunately. My new show compere here and myself are working overtime on the catalogue for the autumn show. Grandfather imported her specially from the U.K., so we've got to justify that and also to show him we can keep on our toes even when he's thousands of miles away.'

The girl Verna said, 'Poor Matt . . . and it's not even your right element, is it? Though you suit it better than

you know. You'll come to terms with it yet ... I'm
quite a prophet. It'll get you even as it got your grandfather.'

He seemed to ignore that, turned and said, 'Miss
Briarley, I'd like you to meet these friends of mine, Mrs
Halley and Miss Verna Halley. Mrs Halley and my
mother went to school together. This is Miss Rosamond
Briarley from Dellabridge's in Southampton. Grandfather saw her give their February Spring showing and
snaffled her. Ideal for her too, as her parents have
settled in Dunedin.'

Rosamond wasn't sure what her boss was up to. Had
he just used that as an excuse or was he going to ask her
to work overtime? ... but if that was so, why had he
taken her from her office for so long? She thought she'd
play it down a little. He'd made her sound like someone
in the top bracket.

She said, 'That's very good for the old ego, Mr
MacQueen, but I doubt if he'd have thought of offering
me a job if it hadn't happened that he knew my grandmother years and years ago. I hope you'll come to my
first show ... I still haven't quite orientated myself to
the seasons here. Autumn in April sounds like something out of a fantasy to me. We're hoping it goes off
well, so that Mr MacQueen feels justified in appointing
me. Mr Matthieu, I must get back to my office now,
excuse me.' She sped away.

He joined her within ten minutes. She looked at him
severely. '*Are* we working overtime?'

He grinned. 'Oh, come, you know perfectly well I was
making that an excuse, though as I like to stick to the
truth as closely as possible, we will. But not here as it's
ridiculous to open up the building for two people. How
about my coming to the flat?'

She raised an eyebrow. 'I'm not even asked if I *can*
work overtime! A sort of royal command, is it? I don't
think——'

'My apologies. I didn't ask if you were free. I thought

that was implicit in "How about my coming to the flat?" Or don't you consider that enough?'

'It so happens I've a man coming to see me on business at seven and I just may have to go out with him for an hour or so. But if you like to make it eight-fifteen, I could be free then.'

'Good. And thanks. I'll bring some folders with me. We could get on much better in an uninterrupted atmosphere. For the same reason, Thelma would like us to have a business discussion at their place before long. Here, of course, she's at the beck and call of both staff and customers.'

'Why not ask her to come tonight? I think it would be a good idea, anyway, to have a third person there.'

He gazed at her in some astonishment. 'You sound quite straitlaced.'

'Maybe I do. It's not a bad thing to be. You can soon get talked about if you entertain your boss in after-hours. And don't look at me like that—I mightn't have meant what you're thinking. It never pays to have any staff member think you have undue influence with the management. I told you I liked being one of the herd.'

'H'm . . . yet you didn't hesitate to spend a whole weekend with my grandfather!'

'That was quite different. He wasn't—then—my boss and we were all of a hemisphere away from the staff.'

Matthieu seemed to enjoy this verbal sparring. He chuckled. 'You don't in the least treat me like a boss, all the same. You don't care tuppence what you say to me, do you? You must be pretty sure of Grandfather and his feelings for you.'

The brown eyes sought his and held them. 'Mr MacQueen, if I regarded you as my permanent boss, I'd be gone now. I'd be in Dunedin with my parents, even if it meant serving behind a counter till I could get into advertising again. I would uphold you in front of my own staff, to the last, as befitting the management, but when you make things so personal, I have to hold my

own. Manse life makes you quite unafraid to speak
your mind. I found an instant rapport with Gaspard.
I'm looking forward to his return, but I don't particularly like *your* attitude. Evidently you don't like
mine ... so that's that.'

She looked for signs of temper, but the tawny eyes
were as audacious as ever. Lines of humour carved
themselves in the brown cheeks as he grinned. 'Oh,
you're mistaken, I *do* like your attitude. I can't stand
boot-lickers, the yes-men and yes-women. Right, I'll see
you later tonight, then. Would you like to take that
sheaf of winter sportswear sketches home with you? No,
I'll take it. I think you walk and they're heavy. Haven't
you got yourself a car yet? Would you like to change
your mind about having a staff car?'

'I haven't changed my mind about it being the wrong
policy to accept privileges like that. And I've something
else to negotiate before I hunt round for a car.'

She saw his lips twitch and almost hated him for his
amusement. She said, 'Well, I'll keep the rest of the
evening free and if you can get Thelma to come with
you, I'd prefer that.' He nodded and left her.

Rosamond hoped desperately that the estate agent who
was calling on her at seven might have something suitable in a flat to show her. She would hate saying
goodbye to this one, with its fragrant garden, and the
treesy riverbank beyond. Nevertheless, she must be
independent. She couldn't afford a flat like this and it
held her back from entertaining the girls she worked
with. There would be gossip, speculation. Matthieu
MacQueen had flatly refused to discuss it with her. He
had said, 'It's entirely over to my grandfather. If that's
the way he wants to run his business I'm not sticking
my neck out. I'll be away again shortly after he gets
back and to upset his arrangements now, for the sake of
your pride or whatever it is, would be asking for
trouble.'

'Why should it be pride?' she asked. 'Why not principle? Common sense?'

'Because I think you want to make a gesture so I no longer suspect you of feathering your nest.'

She had subdued her fury and said mildly, 'I hadn't looked on it as a gesture, and what do your suspicions matter? I want a flat within my means, and my own furniture about me. I can make it plain to your grandfather that you did your best to get me to stay in that one, but that I looked on it entirely as interim accommodation till I could choose my own.'

Now she washed her dishes hurriedly, renewed a vase of flowers, heard a ring at the door, was glad to know the agent was so prompt, and the next moment was gazing in surprise at two men on her doorstep, one the agent, the other Matthieu.

'Oh, Mr MacQueen, I'm afraid I won't be free for ages. I think you must have got me wrong. I'll probably be going out with this gentleman immediately.'

Matthieu shook his head. 'I'm afraid you picked the wrong agent, Miss Briarley. I asked Thelma to come with me, as you suggested, and she told me you were hunting flats tonight. This is the agent I leased this flat from, on behalf of the firm, and I don't think you can have realised the lease is for six months. We don't want it on our hands if you leave. I've explained to Mr Morley that you think it's too expensive, but that my grandfather had specified this type of accommodation. He's been able to tell me what your price range is, so I'll get the accountant at the firm to fix things up so you pay that much for it and the balance can be regarded as my grandfather meant the whole of it to be, as one of the perks with the job. It's often done, when we entice top people out from England. Accommodation guaranteed. When I knew you were looking for somewhere else, I had to ring Mr Morley to find out how we stood over the lease.'

There was just nothing Rosamond could do. She

couldn't make a scene; Matthieu MacQueen was too
well known. The agent grinned, 'You'd have changed
your mind anyway, after you'd seen what I had to offer
at the price. Take what the gods offer, I'd say. We don't
often get people turning down a chance like this. You'd
be crazy to do so.'

She said smoothly, 'Put like that, I suppose I would.
Sorry to have brought you on a wild-goose chase.
Would you like some coffee?'

He accepted with alacrity, which pleased Rosamond.
Given time she would regain her temper. She set the
coffee out on a table in the bay window so they could
admire the sunset, a spectacular one typical of so many
Canterbury sunsets, dyeing the sky behind the pines in
the park across the river with colours surely filched
from Turner's palette. Boats were being sculled up the
river, one or two canoes paddled. 'I find it compensates
me a little for the loss of the Solent. I've taken a canoe
out several times and paddled along.'

'That reminds me,' said Matthieu. 'Thelma would
like you to go across to the harbour with them on
Saturday. The boys want to try you out on their
launch.'

'How kind of them! I'll come gladly.'

'Then I'll pick you up at eleven. Thelma said make it
for lunch.'

She said, 'Why don't I go with them? Isn't there
room?'

His voice was suave. 'It so happens they're going
across Friday night after closing time. And I was going
in any case.'

In front of the agent she had to accept that. She
thought the man would never go. It turned out he had
missed his evening meal through a six o'clock appointment, and he went the rounds of the cookies Rosamond
had put out. Then he departed, happy that the lease
was remaining as it was.

Matthieu saw him out, came back looking, Rosamond thought, self-satisfied and smug. He sat down, looked at her, laughed.

She said, between her teeth, 'Very funny! You had it all your way because he was the agent you'd leased this from. My bad luck. I wish he'd recognised the address when I rang him. I suppose you realise there's nothing to stop me going to another? I'm not bound to stay here.'

'I think you are.' His eyes regarded her steadily and sincerely. 'Because you'll upset Grandfather if you fling this back in his face, and I know you wouldn't like to do that.'

She bit her lip. 'No,' she said finally, 'I couldn't hurt him. I never knew anyone to whom I felt so close in so short a time. Even at the dress show his gaze drew me across the crowded room and in some way, it turned my life upside down.'

'Very apt. They call New Zealand Down Under. It's quite a good thing, at times, to get a new look at the world.'

CHAPTER FOUR

ROSAMOND said, 'Well, if it's work you want, let's get at it. I'm most impressed with your artist. He's so good at these lightning sketches. They'll reproduce most attractively on the catalogue. The only thing is we're rather cramped for time. I wish Thelma had been able to come. We could have got her stuff finalised.'

'Yes, a pity. I should have asked her sooner.'

'You couldn't have. You only invented this on the spur of the moment to dodge an unwelcome invitation.'

'I'd thought of it earlier but hadn't got round to asking you, so it popped into my mind when I needed an excuse.'

'I can't think why. Miss Halley's superbly elegant.
She'd make a terrific model.'.

'She's modelled for us before—does it well too. She
ought to, she's very clothes-conscious.'

'That ought to please the draper in you,' Rosamond
observed.

'It might if I was wholeheartedly a draper, but I can
think of other things more interesting. And Verna
hasn't a lot up top.'

'Do you despise models? Think they're empty-
headed? That's not always true. The best ones have
enough imagination to enhance the creations. Very
often they have a lot of determination and stamina. It's
not as easy as it looks.'

'Oh, Verna has determination all right . . . that's why
I always cut and run.'

Rosamond opened her mouth, but he held up his
hand. 'Now don't, my dear Miss Briarley, I implore
you, tell me I'm the vainest man you've ever met. It
sounds that way I know, but I speak from bitter experience, so don't judge.'

'Why not? You judged me. Even without knowing me
. . . that night in Southampton.'

Surprisingly his eyes fell before hers. He twiddled
with his ballpoint. She added, 'Anyway, I think you're
resourceful enough to make your point with any
woman without having to invent excuses.'

He shrugged. A silence fell. Neither of them seemed
to know where to go from there. Then Rosamond
broke it. 'You aren't a bit like your grandfather . . .
different colouring, different build, even a different way
of looking at things. Perhaps you're more like your
mother's side.'

'No, I'm not. It goes back another generation. I'm
like my father's mother, Gaspard's wife. Talking of
ancestry, was it true what you said, that my grandfather
knew your grandmother? Was she a New Zealander?'

'Yes, but she was very much alone in the world,

and she left here when she was just over twenty. Gaspard must have known her when she was still a student.'

'How did you find it out? Was it just by chance?'

'Not exactly. He saw my name on the catalogue—Rosamond L. Briarley. My grandmother was Louise Rosamond and I'm very like her, so he put two and two together.'

'Aren't likenesses strange?' he commented. 'They can crop out after missing a generation. You're like your grandmother, I'm like mine.'

His grandmother ... the one who'd made the mischief all those years ago and had parted young Gaspard MacQueen and Louise Mellington. Was he like that other mischief-maker in nature as well as looks? She said crisply, 'Let's get at it.'

They worked away for two hours and were very happy with the finished product. When they finally pushed the books aside Matthieu said, smiling, 'We've found a common ground we don't use as a battlefield. Good.'

'Perhaps because it's impersonal,' said Rosamond. 'We ought to keep it that way—avoid all references to anything that happened overseas and keep strictly to business.'

'Sounds dull to me. For instance, I'd like to know where your grandmother and my grandfather met. Do you know?'

'I don't. Gaspard didn't say. I only know it was before he married. My grandmother went off to England and took up a scholarship.' Then she heard herself asking a strange question, far from impersonal, 'Mr MacQueen, were you fond of your grandmother?'

Oddly, he didn't resent it or ask why she wanted to know. He said slowly, 'She was kind, a very good neighbour, full of charitable works, an excellent business woman, but ... I think ... never full of the joy of life as my own mother is. Not the capacity for enjoy-

ment my grandfather has, for that matter. Mother just
bubbles over with it. But perhaps Gran wasn't happy. I
don't know. It mightn't have been her fault.'

'What do you mean?' she queried.

'I never thought she and Grandfather were kindred
spirits. I sometimes wonder if there was something in
their lives that made their marriage less than ideal. In
fact, I've sometimes wondered if he might have gone off
the rails and upset things between them. That could
have soured her, I suppose. It happened before I was
born and I daresay I shouldn't have known about it,
but once, at a funeral, I heard some of the relations
talking about it. It seems that once, long ago, Grandfather went missing for a week.

'These aunts said to each other that Ellie—that was
Gran—had always, afterwards, refused to speculate
about it. It must have been terrible for her. He'd quite
suddenly come home. I was too young then to sense the
implications, but it must have been something like that.'

Rosamond said, 'Had she just got over a big illness?'

He looked positively astounded. 'Yes ... they said
that ... most dramatically. That she'd just been
dragged back from death's door. But what could have
put that into *your* head?'

Rosamond looked and felt confused. 'Oh, I don't
exactly know. You hear about all sorts of things in
manse life. Dad used to say sometimes illness drew
people together, sometimes it thrust them apart.'

Matthieu considered that, a line between the thick
brows. 'It's pretty poor, isn't it? If a man vigorous in his
own health wearies of someone ailing and takes off?
That's not my idea of marriage, or of my parents.'

'Or of *my* parents. Particularly not mine. Dad had
those years of an obscure and crippling disease, like
John Berridge. Mother was still quite young, but it was
wonderful to see them together. I shouldn't have put
that into your mind. There could be some quite un-
complicated reason for it, and she could have known
where he was, but wouldn't tell the gossipy aunts. I

always think that outsiders see the estrangements, but they never see the makings-up.'

She couldn't say to this man who had so misjudged her in her day and generation that in another generation, *his* grandmother had spoiled the young life of *her* grandmother, and that it probably meant that Gaspard, when Ellie had confessed, had felt such bitterness and frustration, he'd taken himself off for a week, to the mountains or the lakes, to get over it. What was a week out of a lifetime? Gaspard hadn't let it break up his homelife.

Matthieu said, 'I'll be glad when this show's over. I wish Grandfather had been back for it. Never mind, he'll be here for the September one. Much more in his line than mine. It's just a weariness of the spirit to me— all that conversation and gush about clothes, all the superlatives, the inane talk. I suppose, though, that you never feel that way. You've come to terms with it . . . or do you still yearn at times after what you first wanted to do with your life?'

Rosamond felt at one with him for the first time ever. It had been kindly said. 'I can't help enjoying marrying words to style and description, but always, about the last hour, I know a great nostalgia for chalky classrooms, for enquiring minds delving into history, for writing poetry and studying it, or even guiding youngsters along those lines. You feel you would be opening doors on life for them. But it doesn't last. I enjoy my career. In drapery.'

'Did marriage never come into it?' he asked.

'Yes, once. It would have brought me to New Zealand, long before I ever dreamed my parents would come here. He was in London, getting experience in hotel management. He had a year to do in Switzerland, and that could have been fabulous—first Switzerland, then here. But Dad got struck down overnight with this complaint. I had to be around, not only because they needed my earnings, but to give Mother a spell with the lifting. So I left university and took a job. Jeffrey had

been trying to persuade me to marry him and have the
year in Switzerland together. It had upset him enough
that I wouldn't stop my studies and do just that, but I
was far too young and needed qualifications.'

'Why didn't he just have that year in Switzerland and
come back to see how things were with your father?'

'It was too indefinite. I did long for him to say just
that, but it was too much to expect really, so we
parted.'

'So now you're wedded to a career in the world of
fashion?'

'Perhaps. I don't really think much about it.'

Matthieu said slowly, 'It could be, if you spend many
weekends in Dunedin, which is the Oxford or Cambridge of New Zealand, you may want to take up your
studies again.' When she didn't reply he said, 'But I
hope not too soon.'

She looked up at him. 'Why?'

His eyes danced. 'Let's say because my grandfather
would probably blame me for losing you to the firm.'

She made a pot of tea, did strips of toast with melted
cheese and snippets of bacon, cut a chocolate ring cake.
For the first time she felt happier about her future with
MacQueen's Ltd. Matthieu understood more of her
background now, and might be prepared, at some more
distant date, to listen to the true story of that weekend
with his grandfather.

She was conscious his eyes rested on her appreciatively now and then. Not that it meant a thing
more than that drapers were always aware of clothes.
She was wearing a deceptively simple-looking emerald
green sponge-cloth suit, with shiny black buttons all
down one side, and it teamed up perfectly with the jet
necklace and bracelet.

When he was going Matthieu said, 'About Saturday
. . . you'll notice that when I'm visiting the Berridges
they all call me Matthieu. In the shop, naturally, it's
formality and Mr Matthieu. Will you do the same?
Sounds a bit stiff otherwise, and on the boat with the

boys it would be out of place. And I shall make it Rosamond.' It was a pity he added, 'Fair Rosamond ... how apt!'

It had been meant as a compliment, but a flake of carnation pink appeared in each cheek. 'No, thank you! That's a drawback to being Rosamond. People will come out with this Fair Rosamond business ...Fair Rosamond was a nasty piece of work in my opinion, the mistress of Henry the Second, who was responsible for Thomas à Becket's murder ... she came to a sticky end, probably at the hands of Henry's wronged Queen Eleanor ... and serve her jolly well right!' Memory of what, in Southampton, this man had believed rose up in her and she added furiously, 'And *I've* never been any man's mistress ... despite ambiguous conversations, Matthieu MacQueen!'

He had actually taken a step backward, then recovered himself. 'Well, who'd have thought it? The cool, sophisticated fashion compere, suddenly a spitfire ... all because I called you Fair Rosamond! Never mind, I like 'em with spirit myself!'

'I don't care what you like. I'm not interested. But I'm not going to be classed with——'

'With kings' mistresses!' To her continuing fury he was laughing helplessly, and she was serious. 'No wonder Grandfather fell for you ... you're fun! Now, don't fly off the handle again and let me try to make my peace. I'm not nearly as history-minded as you are. I'd no idea who Fair Rosamond was—just a term I'd heard somewhere. I'd a vague idea it was some bewitching damsel Walter Scott wrote a poem to.'

She said impatiently, 'That was the lovely Rosabelle. Scott wrote a dirge for her ... she was drowned crossing the stormy firth.'

He scratched his head, looked reflective, then, triumphantly, 'I know ... it was Dark Rosaleen. Now who was *she*? You make me feel an ignoramus! Now what are you laughing at?'

She said, choking, 'You wouldn't have equalled me

with Dark Rosaleen at our first unfortunate glimpse of
each other. That's Mangan's heroine. He called her his
virgin flower! Oh, bother you, I didn't want to laugh. I
was furious with you, and with good cause. You leapt
to conclusions about me, and about your grandfather,
and spoiled what was to be the biggest adventure of my
life to date . . . coming to New Zealand, and frustrated
me tonight in getting a flat within my means, one I
could really call my own . . . and made me work overtime so you could dodge an unwelcome invitation, and
now I feel horribly nervous about your grandfather
coming back. I feel I could be a bone of contention and
I hate disunity in families, and—and——'

He said, 'And I called you by the name of a notori-
ous woman of a long-ago century . . . heavens, I'm no
history expert, but I reckon that was before Magna
Carta . . . and you burst into flames, and now you're
giggling against your will and that makes you madder
than ever.' He grinned and added, 'But it's a good
thing, Rosamond Briarley. That's what I like best about
my parents. I've seen them really spark at each other,
but dissolve into giggles before it got too serious. I've
always thought I'd like a marriage like theirs.'

Rosamond was serious on the instant. She nodded, 'I
know. My parents are like that too.'

They gave each other a long, weighing-up look. They
were slightly embarrassed. They seemed to have got in
deeply. Matthieu said, 'My parents' union is based on
utter trust. It had to be. They've had to be apart for
lengthy spells, and if they hadn't had this faith in each
other it would have been hell.'

'Why were they apart so much?'

'Because Dad's been in Government work without
ever being a Member of Parliament. We're a very mixed
family. I think you know that of the original two brothers, one was a draper and one a farmer. The sons didn't
always follow their fathers . . . at times they followed
their uncles. Sometimes, because they were tough men,
this caused clashes between father and son. Grandfather

didn't force my father to follow him. Dad is a real mixture, went back to the land, gained great experience in that, and during his days in the shop had a first-hand knowledge of trade, so he knew both worlds. He was on so many boards to do with primary produce and what-have-you, he finally became adviser to the Government whichever party was in, and found his true sphere in overseas trading positions.

'Many were of fairly short duration—he went wherever the need was greatest, and as at times this posed problems with my education, my brother's or my sister's, Mother sometimes had to let him go it alone. Then during the school holidays she'd push us off to the farm, where she knew we were blissfully happy, and fly off to Dad. That was only for about four years during our High School days. Then we came up here to Grandfather. Well, I must be off.' With his hand on the door-knob he looked back. 'I'm glad you did laugh. There's a strong bond between my grandfather and myself and I didn't want anything coming between us. Goodnight.'

Saturday was a glorious day, sandwiched in between the weeks of really concentrated work, the strain of the new job, plus the added one of having Matthieu Mac-Queen think there was a highly irregular relationship between her and his grandfather. Since they'd had the flare-up and the subsequent laughter, Rosamond felt he distrusted her less.

The Berridges had gone across to Charteris Bay late on the Friday night. Matthieu called at nine next morning for Rosamond. He looked so different in casual clothes, with a big polo-necked sweater in white pulled over his green shirt and trousers in case of a cool breeze on the water, and he looked appreciatively at her own trim outfit, elegant yet serviceable, biscuit-coloured shirt braided on its sailor collar with brown and gold, and brown tailored trews, belted and buckled. She wore brown and biscuit canvas shoes, and a chunky green sweater that did things for the golden-brown hair curling on her shoulders and the velvety brown eyes.

They wound up through the steep residential area of the Cashmeres, into brown tussocky hills, dotted here and there with great shelter belts of pines that in summer would give shade to scores of grateful hikers.

'Christchurch folk are plains-dwellers in the main,' Matthieu told her, 'so most seem to have a yen to get above the flatlands. So in summer they take to the hills and in winter to the mountains for snow-sports. We've a tramping club at work. Interested?'

'Yes, I'd like that. It seems as if tracks lead all over the hills. Can you go where you like? I notice sheep on the slopes.'

'Yes, anywhere as long as gates are shut. The hills look bare and brown just now, after the long summer with almost drought conditions, but there are still small pockets of native bush tucked into the gullies. You'll see one as we breast the summit by the Kiwi Resting-House, and drop down to the Question Mark Road to Governor's Bay, on the harbour.'

It looked cool and green, with gnarled trees crowded close, and the stream dropping musically from pool to pool over fern-fringed rocks. They didn't turn towards the Port of Lyttelton, close to the open Pacific, but took a road to the right which curved round and over great arms of land like smaller peninsulas within the larger Banks Peninsula, named after Captain Cook's great naturalist. They came at last to a bay where truly golden rock was quarried for ornamental fireplaces and hearths for city homes. The Berridges' weekender was tucked into a tiny private bay, surrounded by evergreen bush, with a cleared space in front of it laid out in lawn, and with masses of yellow daisies and geraniums in great clashes of colour, pink, scarlet, magenta, providing a colourful garden with a minimum of work. It was a brown ranch-type house with white facings on its wide verandahs. Suddenly the last bit of tension fled from Rosamond's so-apprehensive heart. Gaspard's grand-

son had accepted her now, and when the old man returned and Matthieu saw them together, he'd know for
certain that the association had been harmless, born of
the old man's nostalgia for the young love of former
days. But for the fact that it had been Matthieu's own
grandmother who had parted them, the woman Matthieu greatly resembled, she would have told him it had
meant far more to Gaspard than someone he had
merely known in his salad days.

The Berridge family was delightful. Rosamond mar-
velled afresh at the way Barbara treated Matthieu
within the dignified portals of MacQueen's, yet here it
was just the relationship of a young sister and brother.
They laughed at Rosamond because she couldn't remember to call him anything but Mr Matthieu.

'And yet, heaven help me,' he said, 'she seemed to
find it easy to call my grandfather Gaspard.'

Thelma said curiously, 'How would you know that?
You didn't meet Rosamond overseas. I remember you
said you hoped she'd be easy to pick out at the airport
but that you'd probably page her to be sure.'

Matthieu recovered himself quickly, sticking fairly
closely to the truth. 'Oh, I didn't realise it at the time,
but I'd actually glimpsed her. I had some bother tracing
Grandfather. He'd taken off rather suddenly for Southampton, had rung Harry Dellabridge from London and
got invited to the dress show if he could get there. I had
a meal on the way, got to the hotel late, and heard his
voice as I was coming down from being shown to my
room, and here was the old man with a glamorous
damsel who was calling him Gaspard. I didn't know till
I met her at the airport that she was already a pro-
spective staff member to him. I didn't want to reveal to
him I'd spotted him—I thought I could be putting the
old boy in a spot.'

Jerry was young enough to be naïvely surprised.
'What? Old Mr MacQueen? He'd be long past that,
surely . . . falling for someone Rosamond's age . . . why,
he must be seventy if he's a day!'

His father roared. 'I've known some pretty lively seventy-year-olds ... but at seventeen I'd have thought the same as you. It must have given you a shock, Matthieu ... you'd think history was going to repeat itself.' John looked across at Rosamond. 'In the old days the founder of the firm, at eighty, married his secretary and upset the family applecart badly. Courts didn't upset unfair wills in those days and it put the firm on a very rocky footing for a while till some great-great of Matthieu's put it on its feet again. He must have had courage, borrowing a huge sum to buy this woman out. But it paid off. I'm glad it's still a family business, with pioneer roots, and not one of these soulless chain stores.'

At this moment they were coming round under the pine-clad bluffs of Diamond Harbour, a small bay opposite Lyttelton, and under cover of pointing out Godley House, one of the stately homes of the pioneers, Matthieu came close to Rosamond and said, 'That was a ticklish moment ... I didn't want them to know how anti I was at first. Any big department store's a hotbed of gossip, though these folk are pretty safe.'

She looked at him with laughter in her eyes. 'No wonder you said there's no fool like an old fool, when there was an example like this in the family, that old man of eighty leaving his money away and nearly ruining the business.'

He said, still in a low key, 'But not any more. Sorry I gave you such a bad time at first.'

It was not only the sunlight, dancing on the water, that lit her eyes up. She smiled at him. 'It's over and done with. It was an impulse on my part, knowing your grandfather wanted to see the Isle of Wight because of his mother's stories, and my plans were already laid for a weekend there. I'm afraid I was a bit like Jerry. I looked on him as so far on the sere and yellow it never occurred to me anyone could think differently. Mind you, the way he climbed all over the chines made me revise my opinion of age!'

After that the day seemed idyllic ... the sea surely
was a deeper green, the spray that curved from their
wake more dazzling white, the sky bluer, and when they
came back to the holiday house with its private jetty,
and stone steps leading up to that secret garden tucked
into the bush, Rosamond thought she had never heard
bird-song as ecstatic. 'I can pick out thrushes and
blackbirds in it, but there's a note sounding above the
murmur of the water like a bell ... not a tinkling bell
but deep, resonant. Then it stops too suddenly, and I
want to implore it to keep on singing.'

'You've described it very aptly,' said Matthieu. 'It's a
bellbird. If you others go on up,' he added, 'Rosamond
and I will stand quite still, and she can hear the whole
song. It imitates other birds and has quite a range. So
has the *tui*. Only the *tui* clowns a bit and makes guttural
chucklings, but finishes on a harp-like note that to me,
anyway, is purer than any other bird-note. On with
you, folks!'

He had caught her elbow to hold her back. The
others passed them, went on up. All about them was the
shining enamelled green of this tiny pocket of forest, the
soughing of the balsamy pines on the far headland, the
plash of waters from a tiny cascade falling down the
rocks to the sea below ... they stayed perfectly still,
almost holding their breath, not wanting to disturb that
small serenader who had fallen silent. Then it began
again, notes of pure beauty, rising at first as if the small
olive-green bird were flinging them into the air from
sheer joy, then as if purposely dropping them down
through leaf and rock into the curiously green waters
below.

Rosamond's lips were parted, her face uplifted, her
eyes searching the quivering leaves in search of the
source of this exquisite sound. She found it. How could
so small a throat hold a melody like that? A honey-
eater, Thelma had said, and surely its song was the es-

sence of all sweetness. The song finished, the bird flew away, and she turned to thank Matthieu for his patience, but didn't utter any words after all.

His face looked gentler. Gone that forbidding censorious look she had seen when first she had looked up at him. Suddenly she felt embarrassed, freed herself gently and started up the path, Matthieu following closely behind.

They had the evening meal out on the big verandah, then later, scorning television, sat and watched the lights twinkle out in the little bays, saw the beam of a lighthouse, the movements of lighted shipping, the sculpted outline of dark hills against a sky that presently knew the beauty of a full moon rising beyond the hills.

'The next full moon will be the Easter one,' said Matthieu, 'and by then the Show will be a thing of the past. By the way, Rosamond, Verna Halley wants to be in it as a model,' he added. 'She rang me about it yesterday. Okay by you and Thelma?'

Rosamond said, 'Well, that part is over to Thelma, really. She's quite lovely with that colouring, and I was rather disappointed we didn't have a redhead. For autumn, it's lovely. And her hair is the colour of Virginia creeper at its brightest.'

Barbara said bluntly, 'Well, get someone else to do her hair-styling. She rubs me up the wrong way, always picks some flaw. I think she's jealous of our friendship with you, Matthieu.'

'Could be. She's hopelessly spoilt, but fascinating. If she were to marry a no-nonsense man with whom she was madly in love, it'd be the making of her. I don't want to have a rift between the two families because my mother went to school with her mother. One of those curious attractions of opposites, I'd say, though the bond has worn thin by now. Don't make it too obvious, Babs, that you don't want to do her hair. Simply say you're booked out with the other girls.'

Rosamond hoped Verna wouldn't affect the whole

group. Too much temperament was catching. She said so as they drove home.

Matthieu chuckled. 'I've an idea you'd be more than a match for her. You don't stand any nonsense—as witness the way you put me in my place.'

'Oh, Mr Matthieu! I mean Matthieu. Our ... our first clashes were unusual because of the way we first met. I *had* to fight back no matter how wobbly my knees were.'

He was astonished. 'Good grief ... do you mean you were actually scared of me? No one could have sounded less nervous!'

She said soberly, 'You've always been a boss, or the boss's grandson. You wouldn't know. But it was so personal to me that I just about burned to the bone at the very idea.'

They drew to a stop in front of the flats. 'What idea, Rosamond?'

'I knew how it must have sounded when you heard your grandfather say what he did in that Southampton hotel.'

'And you kissed him.' In the light of the street lamp their eyes met.

She said steadily, 'And I kissed him, on the lips. Not just an affectionate kiss on the cheek. But you see that was all tied up with the same thing ... the renewal of his youth. I know how damning it must have sounded, and looked—I'm not an innocent. But the renewal of his youth that he spoke of wasn't a physical thing, Matthieu, a renewal of his physical vigour. It was because in meeting me he'd touched hands with his past, a very romantic past. He and my grandmother had met, loved, quarrelled, parted, and he was thrilled beyond anything to meet me, her granddaughter, as like her as could possibly be, in his own trade. You see, he'd thought she had despised that trade, because he wasn't, academically speaking, her equal. But she hadn't.

'Now I, very little older than Louise had been, was showing him round the places his own mother had

known and loved, told him about when he was a little
lad. I could have been his own granddaughter, born in
her image. So that weekend had held magic for him,
and for me, too.'

'And I spoiled it for you. If only I'd known! I wonder
if I'd barged in, whether he'd have told me about it.
Perhaps not, because he didn't even mention it when he
told me he was engaging a compere but she'd gone on
holiday.'

'I wonder if you can understand this?' said Rosamond. 'A man might be sensitive about telling his
grandson of a former romance. There could be embar-
rassment. Even someone as rugged as Gaspard might
have his tender spots.'

'I think that would be it.' He sat thinking, then, curiously, 'Had you known of your grandmother's attachment?'

'No, it was a complete surprise to me. I don't think
even my mother knows.'

'Then how did you know she didn't feel academically
superior?'

Rosamond caught her breath. She couldn't betray
Gaspard's confidence. After a fractional pause she said,
'Because your grandfather told me that the person who
had made the mischief confessed, too late. By then he
was married and so was Gran. He did take the trouble
to find out—I think he had some vague idea of apolo-
gising to her, but he must have deemed it better to let
sleeping dogs lie.'

'Where is your grandmother?' asked Matthieu.
'Might you ever tell her about it?'

'No.'

'Why not? Oh, is her husband still alive?'

'No ... but I didn't tell Gaspard that. First by accident, then by design, I spoke of Grandfather in the present tense.'

'Why? Now that both of them are free, I don't think I
could have resisted it had it been me.'

She said slowly, 'Because while I think it was a very

strong attachment on Gaspard's side I don't think it
was on Gran's. She spoke to me once of someone she
loved dearly when she was young and something she
said then makes me realise it couldn't have been Gaspard. It must have happened later. But I wouldn't tell
him that. Better to let him have his dream that had that
mischief not been made he and Louise might have married.'

Matthieu turned and grasped her hand, said, 'You
had all that understanding ... it couldn't have been
easy ... you entered into his feelings with great ... oh,
what's the word I want? ... with great sensitivity, and I
spoiled it for you.'

'Oh, not really. Your disgusted look was the look of
a stranger, remember. It didn't hurt beyond a few
moments and I was only glad Gaspard hadn't seen it.
Nothing had tarnished that weekend for him, nothing
ever will. But I admit it was a horrible moment when I
met that same stranger face to face in the airport!'

'It must have been,' he agreed. 'It knocked me for six
in any case, but you'd just travelled across the world.'
He put his elbow on the back of the driving seat, turning to her. 'It was a bad start, Rosamond Briarley, but
we're off to a good one now, I think, don't you?'

Her tone was crisp, businesslike. 'I do, and let's keep
it that way—nothing too personal. It's good to have no
more animosity—good for our business relations, I
mean. But I've always thought business and personal
things should be kept apart. Otherwise staff jealousies
creep in or the two don't mix. One upsets the other.
Thelma's a kindly, hospitable soul, but I think it would
be better for all concerned if I don't take too much
advantage of that. I must tell her she needn't worry
about me being lonely, finding my feet and so on. I
don't think you want your employees cluttering up your
private life too much. I'll fix it.'

His sudden laughs were disconcerting. 'My dear fair
Rosamond ... it's not Thelma you'll have to out-
manoeuvre, it's my revered grandpapa. Like many of

these crusty old buffers he's a real sentimentalist at
heart. I can see how it was . . . he's regarding you as one
of the family. Don't worry, I know you'd never be too
familiar with me in working hours. For goodness' sake,
girl, take it naturally. I can, now I know what it is.
Okay?'

'Um . . . it's okay up to a point, but please remember,
it's not of my seeking.' She sighed.

He flicked her cheek with a careless finger. 'Don't be
so serious over it! After all, my grandfather has never
employed the granddaughter of his long-ago lady-love
before. The old boy'll expect some warmth of welcome.
It'll be a pity if you continue touchy with me.'

She nodded. 'You've a point there. But we're going to
be flat out from now till the show, which is a good thing.
Now thank you for a pleasant day, and goodnight.'

She had the door open before he could move, shut it
quickly and ran up her path.

She did indeed play it cool. Her warning about not
mixing business and personal life hadn't had much
effect. Matthieu asked her out twice in the next fortnight, once to a play put on by a visiting company. She
said, 'As a matter of fact I'm going to see it in a couple
of nights' time, with the head of the hosiery department
and her husband. They're giving me dinner first.'

His eyes crinkled. 'Better watch out! Marigold Dean
is beginning to be afraid that her very attractive son is
going to turn into a confirmed bachelor. I suspect
matchmaking.'

'How horrible of you to tell me! Nothing is more cal-
culated to turn one off. Poor man, he probably suspects
too and will hate me on sight. One always knows.'

'How?'

'By experience. At twenty-five one's had it happen
before. Especially the last three years.'

'You mean since this Jeffrey character let you down?'

'Yes. They gave me a couple of years to see if he'd
come back, then when they heard he'd gone back to

Auckland, they decided it was all off and waded in introducing men into my life. Maddening! When I didn't fancy any of them, they took up the notion that I still carried a torch for Jeffrey. How can you convince people you don't?'

He chuckled. 'The only way is to suddenly fall for someone else. Were you never in danger of doing just that?'

Oh dear, they were back on the too-personal tack. 'No, it's all or nothing with me. I didn't ever feel a vestige of the same feeling, so my career became more and more important to me.'

'So unless——'

She interrupted him. 'Look, you don't pay me for analysing my youthful attractions. I want you to give me your opinion of this. I don't think my wording is really consistent with the Colonial scene.'

'Good heavens, how stilted that sounds!'

'M'm, so does the wording. It wants to be more casual, breezy. Can't you suggest something more natural?'

The next week he asked her out to a dinner-and-dance. Some friends of his wanted a party of six. 'Be my partner for it,' he invited.

'Sorry, I'm too busy. I can't be ready for this show if I don't go over my stuff at home and apart from that, I've a fairly busy week. You have a very friendly staff. If you need a partner, why not Verna Halley? If she dances as well as she walks, she'd really be something. She's a natural as a model.'

He said shortly, 'I'll do my own choosing and asking, thanks,' and she realised he was really angry.

It caused her to flush. She said hotly, 'I told you I preferred to keep business and private life separate ... now you're making me feel I've overstepped the mark. How completely illogical! Can't you see that?'

'I can see that you're getting worked up as the parade approaches. It always happens. I've seen it time and again—it's one of the things that puts me off this life. I'd rather deal with drafting ewes and lambs any day, and they're not easy.'

Rosamond stared at him. He was so equable as a rule, and very patient with the many petty annoyances and rivalries of a big staff. She said, chillingly, 'I think you must be getting a bit het up yourself. I wasn't aware that anything that's just been said had anything to do with the parade. I can't help wishing the invitations I've had recently were from strangers, not from workmates. I never seem to get away from it. That's why I've decided to make Knox Church my church. When I make friends there, it will get me away from MacQueen's Ltd.'

In a sudden change of mood, Matthieu twinkled, 'What a good idea ... it's a very friendly parish. We welcome the stranger in our midst.'

She gasped, 'We? You don't mean that's your church? When I saw you at St Paul's one Sunday I thought that must be it.'

'No, Knox Church is mine and Grandfather's.'

'Then in that case it's St Paul's for me,' and she walked away.

Before she reached the door he said, 'Miss Briarley?'

She turned. 'Yes, Mr Matthieu?'

'I think I ought to tell you that your temper, if not your slip, is showing.'

Their eyes locked and despite her efforts not to, she burst out laughing. But though she hadn't the slightest idea where she was going, she walked out of the office.

CHAPTER FIVE

ROSAMOND found that Verna Halley seemed to be offering friendship. She suspected the girl was rather lonely, occasionally cold-shouldered by the others, slightly suspect because obviously she didn't need to work. They came from a modelling school, she herself was a talented amateur, with occasionally a patronising air.

One night, quite unexpectedly, she dropped in at Rosamond's flat. 'I was out wandering and suddenly realised this was where Matt said you lived. It's really a super apartment. How fortunate that you're able to afford one like this.'

Rosamond decided it might be best to be open rather than secretive. 'Oh, the terms we agreed on amounted to a salary and quarters. I wanted somewhere nice so my parents could come up occasionally to visit me, so we compromised on this. I pay what I'd be charged for an ordinary flat and the firm pays the difference.'

Verna accepted that. 'I gather you'd not tell everyone that. The rag trade is full of petty jealousies. Though with you one of the top experts it oughtn't to matter. I get it too, from the other models. That's why I find you refreshing. When you wholeheartedly praised my looks when I was getting into that copper-bronze suit the other day, I thought, well, here at last is a woman who isn't mean-spirited.'

Rosamond hid a smile. How naïve, an acceptance of the fact that she was probably the most beautiful of any! She said, 'But you'd notice I waited till we were alone. I wouldn't want to undermine any girl's confidence. Quite apart from that, it could make them bitchy with you. I've seen that happen.'

Rosamond made coffee, put out biscuits, answered Verna's questions about her job in Southampton, was careful to let it seem that her encounter with Gaspard MacQueen had been solely a business one.

Verna crossed one elegant leg over the other and leaned back in one of the deep chairs. 'Old Gaspard's having quite a time over there, I believe. He's back from Russia and really living it up in Paris at the moment, Matthieu tells me.'

Rosamond laughed. 'Very easy to appear to live it up in that city! I expect he's with a tour, he's very historically conscious. That's what I gathered from his conversation with my boss. Paris is full of history.'

Verna laughed. 'Not quite what I meant. He's a dark horse.'

Rosamond said lightly, 'Paris sounds that way, but it doesn't have to be. Just as London isn't all strippers and night-clubs. And he's a fair age.'

Verna sounded knowledgeable. 'That's no guarantee. I believed Matthieu himself raised shocked eyebrows over the way his grandfather was carrying on in South-ampton, even. No fool like an old fool, he told Mother and me.'

Rosamond found herself stiffening, felt a slight wave of alarm go over her. Oh, surely Matthieu hadn't been indiscreet to this feather-headed girl? He didn't even like her, or so he'd said.

Before she could think it out, Verna swept on, 'But of course you'd only see the old man in the line of busi-ness.' A thought struck her. 'Wasn't it a bit unusual you getting offered that job? Didn't your boss mind you being approached by another firm?'

'Oh, Mr Dellabridge had known for some time I'd probably come to New Zealand to be with my parents. It was done on a very friendly basis. I was even told that if I couldn't settle, I could return to that job.'

'And will you? I mean, you must miss something about living over there. The close proximity to Europe, for instance.'

Rosamond laughed lightly. 'That's not to be com-pared to being in close proximity to one's parents. But the offer is open.' She went on to talk clothes, some-thing in which Verna was vitally interested. She was glad to get her off the subject of Southampton.

Rosamond felt very restless when she had gone. She hated the thought that Matthieu had talked about that incident. He hadn't known then, of course, that it was perfectly innocent. But now he seemed to have accepted it without a doubt. But how out of character for him to mention it to anyone. She tried to shake off her unease, to tell herself she was getting it out of proportion. The

next few days before the parade were so busy that only
in her leisure moments, mostly tired ones, did the
unease rush back to her.

The parade had gone well from start to finish. The
crowd assembled sensed there was something about this
one that put it well ahead of former shows. There was
an expectancy about them that meant buying, Rosamond knew. The few words of approval Matthieu
managed to inject into her ear now and then were all
the reward she wanted for the long hours over sketches
and wording.

She was conscious she looked her best, once more
clad in the simple cream wool, with the jet jewellery.
She wore a little more make-up than usual, in a clear
coral Barbara had offered, and her hair was styled
beautifully, bringing the golden-brown swirls behind
her ears to be caught at the nape of her neck with a
carved ivory clasp, and with one heavy curl brought
round on to her left shoulder. The afternoon wore on.

There were just two more creations to be displayed in
the evening wear section. For some reason Rosamond
looked back over her shoulder before she passed
through the curtains leading to the dressing-rooms ...
and saw a tall dark figure standing by the glass entrance
next to a huge urn of late dahlias. For a moment she
blinked, sure she'd imagined it, then as the man's eyes
caught and held hers she saw it was indeed Jeffrey
Vane. What ill-luck had brought him here? Had he a
wife viewing the parade?

Suddenly she felt swimmy. She'd not slept well,
strung up with all she knew the day would bring, and it
had been a morning full of nerves, hitches, action. To
her horror, she stumbled a little, regained her balance,
then visibly swayed, just as Matthieu came out of a
door in the narrow passage. He caught her wrist, then
her other shoulder, steadying her, then, very quickly so
no one else could notice, steered her into the room he
had just left, mercifully empty.

He kept hold of her, but lowered her into a chair. 'What is it?' he asked anxiously. 'You've lost all your colour. Sit there, I'll get you something.' This was the tiny room where a bench fridge held cold drinks for the models. He poured a lime-juice, handed it to her. Rosamond sipped at first, then drank deeply, took a tissue, wiped her lips, stood up and said, 'Sorry. I'm perfectly all right now.'

'Are you sure? The crowd's quite happy. The music's playing softly and they're talking about what they'll buy. You aren't appearing again till you feel right on top of things.'

She said, in the tone of one who despises herself, 'It's plainly ridiculous! I suppose because I didn't sleep last night. Jeffrey's out there—the man I used to be engaged to. How can I be so stupid? He doesn't mean a thing to me. I must go. I don't want the girls to know I felt swimmy. It's surprising how catching nerves can be, and these next two models are the cream of the whole collection.'

He nodded. 'I'll keep an eye on you. I'll stand near. Don't push yourself, you can see him afterwards.'

'If I must. The show's all that matters. I'm putting him out of mind right now, blast him.'

Matthieu couldn't help a chuckle. 'I'll walk out with you.'

Rosamond didn't look in Jeffrey's direction, but continued on in her liltingly attractive voice . . . the models appeared, one after another, were greeted with spontaneous applause. Rosamond put her tasselled catalogue down on a small table, spoke her inspired winding-up lines, and was about to walk away when Matthieu stepped forward, took her hand and said, 'This is entirely unrehearsed, and comes as a complete surprise to our new compere from the United Kingdom . . . I heard someone say an hour ago that the compere would make an elegant model herself, and commented on her jewellery. I therefore couldn't resist pointing out that she's wearing earrings, necklace and bracelet of real

Whitby jet, something that's come into fashion again recently, as so many things do, for what is fashion, after all, but a wheel returning?

'Just this morning the costume jewellery department unpacked some simply splendid necklaces that copy Whitby jet as well as any I've ever seen. The head of this firm, Mr Gaspard MacQueen, at present in Paris, no doubt attending other fashion shows, bought these on arrival in England some weeks ago, and they must have been shipped out immediately. They'll be on display downstairs by the time this show is over. I thought no better illustration of the charm of jet could be displayed than here, on MacQueen's Rosamond Briarley, compere of this show. Thank you.'

Rosamond would have been less than feminine if she hadn't felt a great satisfaction at this happening, in front of the man who had failed her so long ago.

History was always repeating itself. Her last show, thirteen thousand miles away, had brought her to New Zealand, through a spectator. What was this one to bring her? She had the maddest feeling she'd like to cut and run. She heard the congratulations of dozens of people, as in a daze, came up against Matthieu. He said, 'I'm near if you want me,' and she flashed him a grateful look. Jeffrey would have enough sense not to approach her while she was still engaged with would-be purchasers. She moved around them with Thelma, and other showroom saleswomen, answering questions, laughing, chatting. She looked supremely unaware of him.

Finally she left a group, and thought she might disappear into the dressing-rooms again, but Jeffrey was at her side, swiftly. She managed to speak before he did, saying lightly, 'Surprise, surprise! I thought I was seeing things, that it must be someone very like you. Then I remembered hearing you'd settled in Auckland. Just here on a visit, Jeffrey? And how in the world did you turn up here? Or have you a wife among this crowd?'

He shook his head. 'No, I'm not married. I came here specially to see you. I saw the advertisement, "Compere: Rosamond Briarley of England", and thought I was seeing things. I'm here on business.'

Matthieu materialised at Rosamond's elbow. 'Hullo, Rosamond. Our big day's over ... the tumult and the shouting dies and I've instructions to bear you off for tea and relaxation. But you appear to have found an old friend. Someone from the U.K., perhaps? Can we press him to join us?'

She said hurriedly and untruthfully, 'I'm afraid he can't spare the time. No, he's a New Zealander, but we knew each other, briefly, in London, years ago. Mr Jeffrey Vane, my employer, Mr Matthieu MacQueen.'

'Interesting,' Matthieu's tone was suave, polite. 'And did I hear you say you're here on business, Mr Vane?'

'Yes, tourist business. I want to buy up some more motels, this time in the South Island.'

Rosamond felt dismayed. Not in Christchurch, she hoped. She would much rather the waters of Cook Strait rolled between her and Jeffrey. She said, 'Well, I'm sorry I can't linger now, but I feel I've earned this break, I just want to flop.'

Her employer nodded. 'Yes, and not in the restaurant. After an outstanding success like this you'd be besieged by people. I've ordered it served in my office. Thelma will be there too. Sorry you can't join us, Mr Vane.'

There was a glint in Jeffrey's dark eyes as he glanced sideways at Rosamond. He had never liked to be involved in awkward situations so he wouldn't try to explain that he *did* have the time, that Rosamond had mistaken him. He said quickly, instead, 'A group of us, all in the tourist industry, are going to the theatre tonight, to *The Middle Watch*, just the sort of thing you like. I'm sure I can get an extra ticket. How about it? I could find out and then ring you. I——'

She had been going to say an unequivocal No, but Matthieu cut in, 'Sorry, but the lady is mine for that.

It's by way of a celebration, for the weeks of work she's put into this, ever since she arrived from Southampton. We're having dinner, then going to the play. Later, as a special celebration, we're phoning my grandfather in Paris ... seeing she was his find, at a show over there, and had the inspiration of bringing her here.'

Jeffrey didn't hide his disappointment. 'I'm leaving for Mount Cook tomorrow. But I'll be back in about ten days or so. Give me your phone number, Ros, and I'll ring you then.'

She couldn't very well refuse that. As he finished writing it down, Matthieu said outrageously, 'And now, darling, you're going to come along and put your feet up ...' He made their excuses to Jeffrey and whisked her away.

As they walked to the lift Rosamond said in a low voice, 'Mr Matthieu, really that was overdoing things! Put my feet up ... it sounded altogether too cosy for an employer.'

'It was meant to. I thought you were going to object to the "darling". Really, Rosamond, you *are* quaint. And what a fellow ... calling you Ros! It's a crime to shorten a lovely name like Rosamond.'

There was no putting up of feet. Thelma was there, the tray in front of her. 'They've done us proud,' she observed, 'and so they jolly well should. That was magnificent!'

When they were done Matthieu said, 'I'll call for you at six-fifteen, Rosamond.'

She'd been sunk in an easy-chair but now sat bolt upright. 'You'll what? But that was only to help me out because you sensed I didn't want to go out with Jeffrey.'

'How could I have known *that*? It was done because *I* didn't want you to go with him. Especially when I had the tickets sitting here. I was going to spring it on you when you were in a good mood and all flushed with success. You've been decidedly tetchy lately about coming out with me.'

She sank back and glanced uneasily at Thelma. He said to Thelma, following her gaze, 'She's got some absurd bee in her bonnet about it not being wise to get involved with the management. Not policy. As if we run our lives by policy, by what's expedient and what isn't! Don't you agree?'

Thelma looked shrewdly at Rosamond and said, 'I expect she wonders what your grandfather will say on his return. I suppose she met him so briefly she doesn't know that although he looks like a chunk of granite, he's got his Achilles heel . . . in fact two, one on each foot, namely his two grandsons, and he wouldn't raise an eyebrow over either of them taking out a staff member. Or in anything else. For instance, in your case, Matthieu, the way he wouldn't insist——'

Matthieu cut in. 'I'll tell her about that some other time, Thelma, if you don't mind. The main thing is she thinks a lot of your opinion, I know, so if you've said so, she'll believe that if Grandfather realises I'm escorting her to a few things, he won't give a damn.'

Rosamond gestured helplessly, 'Carry on talking about me as if I wasn't here. I love it . . . most people do. This is a crazy set-up! I heard years ago that New Zealanders were casual, but I found Jeffrey wasn't. Yet, though this is a formal establishment, with a real sense of family tradition and dignity about it, it seems to be very informal backstage. I suppose I'll have to come.'

'A lovely gracious way of accepting an invitation,' said Matthieu, mock-mournfully. 'I'll pick you up at six-fifteen. And don't go back to your office. I'll send you home in a taxi right now, you can relax for an hour or two, before you start to pretty yourself up.'

She was glad to reach home. She didn't know what to make of Matthieu MacQueen. Was it the volatile French blood in him coming to the top? It seemed odd after his undisguised hostility at first. But by now he seemed to have accepted the fact that the weekend with Gaspard had been just as she had said it was, a purely sentimental one, meant to echo two people he had loved in his past, Rosamond's grandmother, and his own mother. He was always showing her different facets of his personality. At Charteris Bay, in sports clothes, he had looked more like a rugged farmer.

She gave it up, ran a bubble bath, relaxed and began to think happily of what she would wear. Thanks to being in the fashion world, having an excellent salary all to herself now, and with generous staff discounts in her last position and this, her wardrobe, though not extensive, was choice.

This was a brown-and-gold dress for a brown-and-gold girl. It was filmy, with long brown sleeves through which a gold bracelet glinted, and the rest of it carried the gold glint in every movement of the tiered skirt that looked pencil-slim, it was so finely pleated, till it fanned out with her movements. It was low-cut and her one piece of really good jewellery, a single topaz, set in a modern coil of gold wire, lay against her creamy skin and she had golden tasselled earrings swinging at her ears. Barbara's hair-styling suited this dress. She had a brown velvet jacket, simplicity in itself, to go over it, because these March nights were becoming tinged with a hint of autumn frost now.

Matthieu stopped halfway across the room to her as she turned from gazing out of the window. 'Very lovely indeed,' he said. 'I can't think why we don't use you as a model.'

She laughed, 'Because I'm more useful describing creations on other girls, and besides, I couldn't.'

'Why not, you've certainly got what it takes.'

She dimpled. 'But one grave drawback. I wouldn't be able to help giggling.'

He laughed back at her. 'I believe that. You're too sincere to simper. Or if that isn't fair to those models we used, too sincere to take yourself seriously. Now, let's forget the world of fashion and just enjoy ourselves. I've seen *The Middle Watch* twice before, but it comes up freshly every time.'

She nodded. 'Dad has the book in his library and I've read that twice. I'm looking forward to it.'

He said abruptly, 'I'm going to ask you something straight out. Does this Jeffrey fellow mean anything to you, *now*? I mean, is it just satisfaction at showing him he's not the only pebble on the beach ... that he can't just barge in again and pick you up now you're free from family obligations, that you went along with what I sprang on you? Or what?'

Her lips twitched. 'You surprise me about every ten seconds we're together, Matthieu. Mind if I ask you as candid a question first? Why did you do it? Just an impulsive gesture of chivalry because I threw a wobbly when I saw him? Or what?'

'Damned if I know. It was purely instinctive. I had a sudden primitive urge to slap the fellow down. And I hated the fact that his sudden appearance made you go weak at the knees. Going to answer me as frankly?'

'Yes, you deserve that. I was surprised myself at my reaction. But it was mostly temper. I was simply furious that he turned up there and then when I didn't want anything to distract me. A show is a big strain, and quite apart from that I didn't want to see him again, ever. He was abominably selfish when Dad was so ill, thought only of how it would affect him. He's just a reminder of how undiscriminating I was at that age. But ...' she grinned, 'I've got to confess I knew a great feminine satisfaction that you so deftly spiked his guns. It was one of the most satisfying moments of my life.'

He chuckled. 'Very honest ... but tell me, just as truthfully, seeing he'll be at the theatre, is this lovely dress for his benefit, or mine?'

When sparks appeared in her eyes they lost their velvety look immediately. 'What a horrible thought! It's for you, of course. You're the one who's so knowledgeable about fashion, not Jeffrey. You're an expert. What girl wouldn't take pains with her appearance going out

with you? You can appreciate fabric, design, everything.'

He held up a hand. 'Don't eat me! I took a risk
asking. Rosamond, if your grandmother was half as
endearingly ready to go off half-cocked as you are I
don't wonder my grandfather fell for her. Come on, my
girl.'

Rosamond was feeling just as weak at the knees as
she had when she saw Jeffrey across that crowded
room. Only this was rather a delicious weakness, an
absence of all tension, as if nothing mattered except the
present.

They were settled a few moments before Jeffrey's
party came in. They were just across the aisle from
them. Jeffrey came over, leant across Matthieu who was
in the aisle seat, said, 'There's just a moment to the
curtain . . . worst of being with a crowd, it takes ages to
get organised, but see me afterwards. Perhaps I could
take you both to supper?'

Matthieu's voice held a drawl. 'Sorry, we've something jacked up. Sorry not to invite you along, but it
can't be done. We'll go out to the vestibule in the interval, though, to see you.'

When Jeffrey had gone back to his seat, Rosamond
touched her hand to Matthieu's, meaning it to be a
brief gesture of thanks. He turned his over it immediately and engulfed it in a swift movement. She
said, 'I just wanted to say thank you.'

His eyes glinted audaciously, 'And for myself, I just
wanted to hold your hand. I thought it nice that we
appeared, for once, to be two minds with but a single
thought.'

She gave him a quelling look but left her hand in his.
Then she said, 'How strange . . . your hands aren't like
a draper's hands at all . . . your palms are calloused.'

'Have you had a long experience of holding hands
with drapers?'

'Idiot! I suppose, anyway, you garden a lot?'

'Well, I do just now. We have only a part-time gardener and at present I have to keep Pierre's garden up to scratch too. You must come round and see my prize dahlias some time ... at least Grandfather's. Ah, it's starting.'

Rosamond wouldn't have been a woman had she not enjoyed the brief encounter with Jeffrey during the interval. Jeffrey was treading carefully. His eyes, roving over Rosamond's elegance, said what he dared not say with her escort, and boss, there.

'What made you come to New Zealand, Rosamond?'

She looked surprised. 'Matthieu told you this afternoon. His grandfather saw me compere a show in Southampton and brought me out here.'

Jeffrey shook his head. 'I mean, once you thought New Zealand at the uttermost ends of the earth ... changed your mind?'

'It was too far then, when my father was so ill ... but now he's so wonderfully restored, *and* in a Dunedin parish, New Zealand was the lodestar that drew me.'

Matthieu added, 'She's leaving the best bit out. My grandfather and Rosamond's grandmother were sweethearts long ago ... I was in Southampton with my grandfather. Our powers of persuasion proved too much for the dear girl.' Matthieu was being outrageous, Rosamond thought. He just couldn't resist embroidering the truth.

Jeffrey said, 'How splendid that your father recovered so completely.'

Rosamond said deliberately, 'It cost a lot but was like a miracle. It was a family effort. My brother provided most of the finance. My money helped, but most of all, I was there to help Mother with the nursing. Now all sorts of lovely things are happening. My brother will probably be in New Zealand by the end of the year.'

Matthieu added, 'And Rosamond and I are even thinking of getting her grandmother out to New Zealand to meet her long-ago sweetheart.'

Jeffrey said rather stiffly, 'It all sounds quite idyllic.'
There was little time left. He said quickly, 'Anyway,
Rosamond, I'll ring you when we get back from
Queenstown, or call at the shop.'

She said, just as quickly, 'Make it a ring at home. It's
against policy, as in all businesses, to have too many
personal contacts in trading hours.'

'Even if you're on a different footing from most of
the staff,' Matthieu couldn't help adding. 'Well, that's it
... back into the theatre.'

The comedy was so lighthearted, so timelessly hilarious and well acted, that Rosamond's spirits were cloud-
high by the time the curtain fell. She was glad when the
accountant from the firm, with his wife, came up to
them in the aisle. This meant she could just nod to Jeffrey in a goodnight gesture.

Mr Yelland said, 'Have you rung your grandfather
yet?'

Matthieu was quite open about it. 'No, I felt we
couldn't get the old boy up too early. I left a call in for
him and I'm taking it at Rosamond's flat. We're having
supper there.'

Rosamond acted quickly. 'How about you two
coming too? Then if the call's delayed, it will help to
pass the time. These international calls are often
chancy. It'll be a plain snack because I didn't know this
was happening till I got to the theatre, but I'd love to
have you.'

Cicely Yelland said promptly, 'We'll come. Don's
such a one for rushing me home and I'd love to talk it
over with you.'

Her husband groaned. 'And it cost me a pretty penny
too, I might tell you. Cicely got carried away ... but
she doesn't often, I grant you.'

As Matthieu handed Rosamond into his car he said,
'Very neatly done, dear girl. You think I'm making the
pace too hot, don't you?'

He drove off. She said, 'I told you I didn't think it
good policy. One moment you're furious I'm here; now

you're rushing me off my feet. It's risky. It was kind of you to give me a boost in front of Jeffrey, but it wasn't necessary to mention supper at my flat after the show to your accountant and his wife. You might recall, from the conclusions you jumped to in Southampton, that it's disastrously easy to give the wrong impression.'

He said mildly, 'I expect it's from living in manses so long.'

'What is? You mean sounding straitlaced? Well, it's not a bad idea to be——'

'I didn't mean that. I mean the way you put words together. That last sentence sounded like something from a sermon.'

She said, 'You're hopeless!' then found herself laughing. 'I was trying to sound stiff, to make you remember you're my employer and I'm just someone on your wage-bill. I'd like it to stay that way.'

He glanced at her quickly, then turned his gaze back to the road. 'Would you, Rosamond? Would you really?'

'Yes, I would. *Really!*' She said it far too quickly and with too much emphasis. He didn't answer. The short journey was over.

She felt more normal as she prepared some light refreshments. She found half a dozen savouries in one tin, fortunately, patties made from rounds of bread pressed into patty-pans butter side down and filled with mashed potato and salmon. She popped them into her oven to heat, made some tomato sandwiches, hunted out some squares of marshmallow cake she'd made for Thelma's boys last Saturday, and some shortbread. This week had been far too hectic to think of baking, but at least this filled four plates.

They had just finished nibbling when the call came through. Matthieu talked first, reporting on things other than the fashion show, then waxed lyrical over it, in a way that made Rosamond's cheeks grow warm. Cicely laughed at her in the nicest way, 'Isn't it odd how shy we are over praise? But you deserve every

word.' Matthieu held out the phone to Rosamond.
'He's thrilled you're here, is dying to speak to you.'

She felt everyone could hear him as he boomed,
'Dear girl, it's good to hear your voice again! From
what my grandson tells me everything is going splen-
didly. I'm rather sorry I planned so long a trip now,
but I'll go through with it. I've been able to see a lot
more than just high fashion, fortunately. We Mac-
Queens, with the exception of Pierre, remain farmers at
heart, and I managed to get right out into the countryside here, and in Russia. Tell me, Rosamond, have
you told your grandmother who you're working for
yet?'

She thought his voice had lowered. 'No, not yet, Gaspard, but I'll be telling her in my next letter. I sent her a
letter from England saying I was off to a firm in Christchurch, but I didn't mention the name. I don't think I'll
let on I know that you knew her. I feel I'd like *her* to
tell *me* she knew you long ago. Can you understand
that, Gaspard?'

There was a short silence, then, 'I can, Rosamond
Louise. I've been impatient for her to know, but I've
got to realise it may not be as important to her as to
me. I'll leave it to you.'

Rosamond thought she should change the subject,
make it less personal. 'Mr and Mrs Yelland are here.
Would you like to speak to Mr Yelland?'

'I would . . . especially as young Matthieu is paying
for the call . . . he assured me he had it charged to his
number. In fact, put Cicely on too. I'm sure it would
give her a thrill to speak to Paris from New Zealand.
Goodbye for now, darling girl, keep well and happy.'

Cicely was surprised and sparkling-eyed when Rosamond held the phone out to her, they chatted, then Mr
Yelland took it and went into facts and figures.

Cicely had a curious air about her when it was
finished. Matthieu noticed it and gratified it immediately. 'You've gathered that there's a link between
my grandfather and Rosamond's grandmother. The ori-

ginal Rosamond . . . who was Louise Rosamond, to be
exact . . . was so like our Miss Briarley at her age, or a
little younger, that Grandfather recognised the relationship when he attended this parade in Southampton.
Apart from that, he was so impressed with her work, he
engaged her right away.'

Rosamond said, 'She was only twenty. Five years
younger.'

Matthieu nodded. 'Must have been. Grandfather
married at twenty-two.'

Cicely said, 'I scent a romance . . . was it?'

Don Yelland groaned. 'Here she goes! Watch out,
Miss Briarley. My wife's a born matchmaker. She'll
probably kid round you to get your grandmother out
here and try to breathe life into the dead ashes. I take it
she's a widow, is she?'

Matthieu answered for her. 'She is, but Rosamond's
a spoilsport, hasn't told Grandfather that yet. But I'll
tell him.'

Rosamond was glad the subject was dropped when
Don Yelland said, 'Mr MacQueen said you were on no
account to skip that trip to Australia, Matthieu. He
said it's just as important to you as fashion shows to
him, and that if you waited till Pierre and Natalie got
back, it could put you back a year. He said anyone can
be spared for ten days. I never thought the day would
come when the Old Man would admit that. So you
must go, we'll manage fine.'

Cicely managed to manoeuvre Don to the point of
leaving. 'He's hard to get out, but harder still to dislodge once he gets settled in at anyone's place, and he
looks all set to discuss shop till the early hours, and Mr
Matthieu won't want us here all that time.'

Rosamond could have choked Matthieu when he
said, 'Very tactful, Cicely, but Miss Briarley of Mac-
Queen's is a great stickler for the conventions. I'm
never allowed to stay late. She has a real genius for
speeding the parting guest without offending. Comes
from living in a manse.'

'Very sensible too,' said Don Yelland. 'We meet up with that attitude all too seldom these days . . . and so, goodnight.'

Matthieu chuckled as soon as the door shut behind them. 'You'd notice Cicely didn't endorse that. I don't think she was so much matchmaking in our grandparents' direction as in ours and——'

'That will do, Matthieu,' Rosamond put in. 'You're in a mad, mad mood and I must save you from your reckless self. What a pity you don't wear a hat. If you did, I could just pick it up and hand it to you and you'd have to go.'

He looked at her reproachfully. 'After all my efforts at saving you from the pressing attentions of Mr Jeffrey Vane! I might just as well not have rescued you for all I'm getting in the way of thanks.'

Her eyes challenged him. 'What were you expecting? A five-minute speech, or a framed testimonial for chivalry?'

The challenge was met. 'No . . . just this . . . the nicest reward of all.' He seized her, in all her loveliness of brown gauzy draperies, shot with gold, caught her against him, bent his head . . . his mouth came down on hers, his lips cool at first, then warming.

He lifted his mouth after a while, said against her lips, 'Don't *you* think it's nice too?' and went on kissing her.

Rosamond felt as if time itself was suspended. Since Jeffrey had proved so selfish she had shied away from incidents like these, had made herself content with work, and friends, and simple pleasures . . . had forgotten the overwhelming magic of such moments. The fact that she could think this, admit it to herself while still within the intimacy of his embrace, brought her to her senses. She stirred a little in his hold and withdrew slightly. Matthieu let her withdraw, said with a whimsical lift of the brow, 'Don't you want to prolong this? Now, be your usual honest self, Rosamond Briarley, don't you?'

The brown eyes met the tawny ones quite candidly. 'I think I'll admit I do ... I'm not made of marble ... but I don't really think it's wise!'

His laugh had pure merriment in it. 'Oh, what a funny darling girl you are! Funny, but sweet. That'll do to be going on with. And, Rosamond, drop this nonsense about policy and management and staff ... there's just you ... and me ... and something that happened long ago for an extra touch of romance. I'm all in favour of history repeating itself.' And he was gone, still laughing.

CHAPTER SIX

FORTUNATELY the next day was taken up with catching up on departmental ads that had taken second place to the parade. How much easier life would be if the more tender side was kept quite separate from business hours. However, Matthieu's manner next morning was extremely brisk, not betraying in any way that there had been a romantic interlude between them the night before. He seemed to have the power of switching off. Rosamond was glad of this. She saw little of him in any case.

Towards four she had to take a sheaf of small ads to his office. She'd seen his shadow through frosted glass, leaving one of the bigger offices outside his own a few moments before, and thought she'd slip in with these while the office was empty. She didn't want to appear to be looking for a follow-up to their warmer exchanges of the night before. Or to be asked out. She needn't have worried.

She was about to go into his office when she heard his voice. He must have been called back to the phone. She paused. His voice said, 'Oh, I see. Well, it won't matter, Mrs Halley. I'll call for Verna instead, at eight. It'll be a late affair, I think. Yes, it was a good show, wasn't it? Verna looked ravishing in the green, and in the black too. Nothing like black for a redhead. I don't suppose I'll see you tonight, it'll be so late, but I'll certainly be at your dinner-party Saturday night. I——'

Rosamond decided not to wait any longer. She turned, said to his secretary, 'Shona, Mr Matthieu's on the phone and I haven't time to wait. Would you give him these and ask him to mark which of the haberdashery ones he prefers, and return them? Thanks.'

She curled her lip as she walked back. If he wanted to get away from Verna he wasn't running very fast, was he?

Last night she had lain awake quite a long time, because she had been disturbed by all sorts of longings, thrilled by something unexpectedly sweet ... Rosamond, it's a lot of moonshine, you're just carried away by the romance of what happened long ago between two other people ... how sentimental can you get? And you were elated because he put Jeffrey in his place so satisfyingly. Don't make another error of judgment, in the mood of exaltation you were in because the parade was so successful!

He asked her, the following day, if she would like to have a run up to Porter's Pass, among the mountains of the Great Divide, on Sunday. 'We could leave early, take a picnic lunch, and be back for church at night as befitting a daughter of the manse. I think you'd love it.'

She said, with only the politest note of regret in her voice, 'Oh, sorry, Monica's fiancé is coming down, and she asked me to go with them, and her brother, to Lake Coleridge. I believe it's very lovely. Sorry, Matthieu, some other time perhaps.'

'It is lovely. That was another spot I promised myself I'd show you, along with others within easy reach ... Akaroa, our nearest French-settled town, Peel Forest, Ashley Gorge ... later, in winter, to the snow-sports

areas. Don't tie yourself up too much, will you?' And
he was gone, supremely confident that she'd leave most
of her time free for him.

Surprisingly, Verna called in one night soon after,
took Rosamond for a drive to the beach, where at New
Brighton heavy surf pounded up to miles of sandhills,
and the curving shore swept north, many miles distant,
to the mountains of the Kaikoura Ranges.

'Pity daylight saving is finished,' said Verna, 'the
evenings are too short now for much of this, but we'll
run back to our place. The view is quite stupendous.
We're on the Cashmeres.'

There was no lack of money here. It was beautiful
but a little overpowering. The whole house looked as if
it had been designed and furnished by an interior decorator, and nothing had been kept for sentiment's sake
except valuable antiques. There was something quite
soulless about it . . . what? Suddenly she realised it was
a lack of books.

Nothing, not even those exquisite cabinets filled with
treasures of china and crystal, the good paintings, some
choice prints, could make up for shelves of well-read
shabby books. There wasn't as much as a pair of book-
ends supporting half a dozen books in the living-room.

Verna herself was flawlessly beautiful, but there
wasn't enough variety in her conversation . . . that
would be because she didn't read. She was wrapped up
in herself, yet she was curiously sweet to Rosamond.
And very candid. 'You've got what I haven't . . . you
can stand on your own feet. I daresay I've been hopelessly spoiled, but I have the knack of making life very
pleasant for other people, so that's something, I suppose.' She giggled. Rosamond couldn't help liking her.

When they were leaning on an upstairs balcony rail,
watching the glorious spread of lights below, in the city,
Verna said, 'Would you think me frightfully cheeky if I
asked who that man was the day of the show? You
seemed to know him . . . is he from England? Has he
followed you here? Does he mean anything to you?'

She *was* naïve; Rosamond responded. 'Jeffrey Vale? I was once engaged to him. He's in the hotel and motel business, he has some in Auckland and he's looking for some in the South Island.'

'Why didn't you marry? Or is that going too far?'

'I don't mind a bit. My father was very ill and they needed me at home. Needed my money too. Jeff's very self-centred. He wanted me to go to Switzerland with him—he was having experience there. I was just infatuated. My fancy for him died a sudden death.'

'How beastly! Does he want to make a comeback now?'

'He did. But I made it plain there's nothing doing.'

'Very wise. Well, I wish you better luck next time. Trouble is, or so I've heard, one tends to fall for the same sort of guy over and over again. So watch it ... do some analysing next time. Don't make the mistake of falling for a man as utterly selfish as Matthieu Mac-Queen! I did once, a long time ago, but fortunately my eyes were opened in time. Mother still cherishes hopes ... but not for me, thanks. It's embarrassing, though.'

Rosamond was so astonished, she exclaimed, 'Matthieu? Selfish? Oh, surely not. He seems more inclined to be quixotic. He rescued me very neatly from Jeff the other day.'

'He seems that way, but there's always method in his madness. A cunning, underhand devil. I sometimes get cross the way he panders to his grandfather. The old man likes brains as well as looks in women. Pierre tried to live his own life, but the old man interfered.'

'I heard the opposite from that, but perhaps I got it wrong. But what modern male allows himself to be put off the girl he wants to marry? Is that what you meant?'

'Well, there's a lot at stake. Old Gaspard is the piper who calls the tune. He's of another age and generation. Have you any idea what that business is worth? Matthieu would go along with the old man that way too, I'm sure.'

Rosamond knew she must steer the conversation

away from Matthieu. She said, 'But Pierre and Natalie are spoken of as ideally suited.'

'It certainly seems that way—and sure did to the old man. Natalie is the apple of old Gaspard's eye. He practically engineered the match. Pierre is managing director of MacQueen's, Gaspard is the leading director. He didn't want anyone as flibbertigibbet as the first girl Pierre fancied; she was a big spender and would have run through a wad in no time. So he very adroitly broke it off . . . and saw Natalie was around to pick up the pieces.

'Then Matthieu . . . he hasn't got his heart in drapery, but look at him . . . comes running every time the old man whistles. He knows which side his bread is buttered. He'll always go along with what Gaspard wants—he'd be a fool not to. Oh, dear, I'm gossiping. Rosamond, don't think any the less of me for this, it's just that I'd hate to see you hurt. Especially if you've been hurt badly once before.' She smiled, quite nicely. 'I do so want you for a friend. I've never found it easy to make friends. Sounds corny, but I'm the perfect little lonely rich girl type. We always had so much more than the girls I went to school and college with, and it doesn't make for easy friendships. But I feel you're different. Is it because your father was a minister and you had to mix with people in all walks of life?

Rosamond laughed. 'Could be. Our parishes were always mixed. I've never thought much about it because I didn't need to, but I can see that in your case it could make for loneliness. You could have girls rather conscious they couldn't offer you the same sort of hospitality. I mean, if you put on slap-up dinners for them, and they felt all they could offer was sitting round in student flats on cushions on the floor with mugs of coffee and plates of spaghetti, they wouldn't be very forthcoming. We often entertained people much better off than we were, but they just accepted us as we were.'

Verna looked around her. 'Of course this is Mother's home—not the same as having a flat of my own. You're

lucky now ... having the sort of flat you've got. Old
Gaspard must have really fallen for you.'

Rosamond felt a faint feathering of unease run over
her. She said, calmly enough, with a slight laugh, 'It
was just an inducement for me to leave Dellabridge's.
Salary *and* accommodation. And as I told you, he just
pays the difference between what I'd pay myself, and
that luxury flat.'

Verna nodded, seemingly accepting that. 'It's only
that the MacQueens rarely do things solely out of good-
heartedness. They're tough hombres really. Just watch
it. I used to think Matthieu was marvellous, but not
now. Mother will never see through them. I'm a little
more shrewd, I take after my father. He was very far-
seeing.'

Rosamond lay awake for an hour that night, thinking. Verna had sounded quite sincere. She thought she
would walk warily. It was a tricky situation. She
wouldn't want to be manoeuvred, even by someone as
lovable, to her, as Gaspard MacQueen. If Verna meant
he'd steered Pierre into a suitable marriage, he was
quite capable of edging Matthieu his way. Odd, she
wouldn't have thought Matthieu could be manipulated.
She wouldn't have thought him selfish either.

Well, whatever they were up to, grandfather or grandson, it was as well she'd already intimated that she
didn't think it wise for an employee to become involved
emotionally with the heads of the firm. She was glad
she'd turned down some outings with him. How come,
though, if Verna didn't really like him, that she'd been
going out with him? ... and then there was the dinner-
party. Still, if Verna's mother wanted it, no doubt
Verna had to go along with it to a certain extent out of
sheer politeness. Matthieu had said his mother and
Verna's had been school friends. But she'd watch her
step.

The following week she was unable to dodge an invitation. Besides, she had to admit to herself she didn't
want to. Matthieu asked her to dinner at his grand-

father's house. He didn't have a flat of his own, that much she knew. 'The Humphreys keep house for Grandfather, have for years,' he told her. 'Humphrey still works at his own job and helps me keep the grounds right, and Goldie, his wife, looks after us. Grandfather writes her regularly, has told her about you, and she's dying to meet you. They were away down south visiting their daughter at the time of the show and I was baching, so Goldie didn't meet you there. They'll have dinner with us. It can be whatever day suits you, so how about it?'

Rosamond opted for Thursday. It would be interesting. Perhaps Goldie would give some hint if Gaspard was indeed entertaining any matchmaking ideas. She would go with an open mind.

As Matthieu had said, when she arrived, it was not far from her flat, one of the big houses backing on to the Millbrook Reserve, on the banks of the river, a copsy place that held a wishing-well and leafy paths where in spring crocuses in white, gold, and blue lifted dewy chalices to the sun, and in autumn maples and oaks and poplars made scarlet and russet and gold patches amid the green.

The house was named Shanklin for Gaspard's mother. In the garden Rosamond was delighted to find a fernery cut deeply into the ground to allow a small stream to trickle its way to the Reserve. At the side of it were rocky steps, crevice-sweet with ferns and purple alyssum, mint and thrift. Tree-ferns were twelve feet high, to keep it moist even in the hottest of summers, and to look up through their starry symmetry to the darkening sky was enchantment in itself, like a fairy grotto from the land of childhood.

Rosamond said so, eyes wide and sparkling. 'It's like Shanklin Chine in miniature. Did your great-grandmother plan it that way, Matthieu?'

'My great-grandfather planned it for her.'

'You wouldn't have known her?'

'I have one memory, and it's of this very spot. I was very small. She brought me here and made me little boats out of that bamboo on the bank. She was very good at it. She sat on one of the stones. I thought it funny that for a grown-up she didn't mind getting her clothes wet or reminded me I shouldn't splash so much. It went on all afternoon. We put them in the top pool, prodded them with long bits of bamboo, let them go right down. I had to run to the bottom and rescue them before they went under the fence.

'Years afterwards I asked who was the lady who'd made me bamboo boats that day. They all gaped at me, unable to believe I could have remembered it. Grandfather was quite excited I could remember his mother. He said it was the day of the funeral of my baby sister, and Great-Granny thought that was something she could do, keep the youngest amused and from worrying my parents. My sister was only three weeks old.'

Rosamond felt deeply moved. She could see the old lady, wise in her day and generation, not wanting a sorrow he couldn't understand to touch the youngest child. She could remember the Shanklin Chine of her own childhood here in miniature. Matthieu heard her swallow.

She said, 'I'm so glad you can remember her. How lovely for Gaspard to know you'll be able to tell your own children some day that you can remember someone as far back in time as that. I suppose it's because history was my subject, but there's something magical in touching hands with the past. How old was she then?'

'About ninety. She died soon after.'

'Then she must have been born in ... um ... let me see ...'

'In 1865.'

'1865 ... how incredible, to think that your life and hers met and touched! I take it that your grandfather must have been born late in life to her? Yes. Matthieu

... let me think ... that was in the first half of Queen Victoria's reign and ... yes, the very year Lincoln was assassinated. How fantastic it seems!'

He laughed at her enthusiasm. 'And since then the aeroplane has come into its own and we can cross the world in little more than a day, which was the only reason I could take off to see Grandfather the traumatic time of our first encounter.' He chuckled reminiscently, 'Never did I guess then I'd be sitting here with you, talking about my great-granny. Oh, that's Goldie calling. She approves of you. I told her you'd a splendid appetite and didn't have to watch calories. She gets frustrated about the slimmers. When you suggested I show you the garden while she got on with the last touches to the meal, she whispered to me that you had gumption as well as looks, that she can't abide the ones who flutter round the kitchen and make the dishing-up take longer.'

Rosamond was aware that both the Humphreys were weighing her up. As if they held a brief for the absent Gaspard so they could report on any females on his grandson's horizon. She liked them so much she relaxed and forgot about it.

Goldie was evidently an experimental cook, not in the least conservative, and from the way Matthieu teased, every week she tried out at least one new recipe from an English magazine she was addicted to. 'Though some are pure New Zealand, as you'll see when we come to the dessert. It's passionfruit cream.'

Goldie said tartly, 'You aren't supposed to tell guests what's coming. We've got no further than the soup.' It was a delicious creamed one, chilled, cucumber, celery, parsley, and the green Wedgwood jugs on the dinner-table matched the green of the herbs and the gingham design on the edges of the bowls it was served in.

The entree had been made the day before, Goldie revealed, and refrigerated, then heated up ... wafer-thin pancakes rolled up with a filling of flaked fish, *terakihi*, in a spiced sauce, decorated with button mushrooms. 'I might as well tell you the rest, or Matthieu will. It would be said to originate in Scotland, and has been a favourite with generations of MacQueens. They came from Strathdearn, so we call it the Strathdearn Roast. It's just a saddle of mutton, served with redcurrant jelly instead of mint sauce.'

Matthieu took it up. 'Hogget mutton, in our family's opinion more mellow and flavoury than lamb, and homegrown. No deterioration from hours being trucked to the works and fed on lakeland pastures.'

Goldie chuckled. 'The lad's beginning to sound like one of his own ads! There's more of the draper in you than I'd suspected. Or is some of Miss Briarley's expertise rubbing off on you?'

'I can tell you what *is* rubbing off, Goldie, and that's her ruling passion for history. We were talking of my great-grandmama, and she asked when she was born and rattled off things about this and that happening in 1865 till I felt an ignoramus. Reminds me of that poem ... what was it, and who was it by? You know ...

"and still they gazed, and still the wonder grew
    That one small head could carry all he knew." '

Rosamond dimpled, 'It's *The Village Schoolmaster*, by Goldsmith.'

He shrugged. 'See what I mean ... enough to give a fellow an inferiority complex!'

'How absurd ... it's just a matter of early training. You leave me behind in other fields. The other day when you called me in when you had some travellers there, I felt you knew more about those fabrics than they did. You knew everything from the raw fleece up, and despite having spent so many years in the same trade, I felt an ignoramus then.'

George Humphrey said, 'Well, you wouldn't expect to know it as well as someone brought up in the mixed tradition of the sheep-farming-cum-drapery family of the MacQueens. Not many in the trade can boast of having shorn sheep.'

That would explain the callouses in his palms. He

must often go to his sister's farm. She said, 'I notice you shrugged just then. For the first time I could see a trace of those French ancestors Gaspard spoke about. I've seen it in French descendants on the Channel Islands as well as on the Isle of Wight. Till now, to me, you've looked pure Scots.'

'She's got the seeing eye all right,' said Goldie. 'Too few remember the old lady. Margot Somers she was before she wed, a name anglicised from St Omer. At first glance Matthieu is like Ellie, but every gesture is Margot. And rightly so. How she loved that little boy!'

'Goldie, watch it!' warned Matthieu. 'I'm Rosamond's boss. It will undermine my authority if you start getting all sentimental about my first tooth and my crop of golden curls.'

'Golden curls? You had nothing but a stubble. And as you aren't in the habit of bringing home employees, I wasn't looking on her in that light.'

'Not bringing—what about Thelma and Barbara and——'

'You ken fine what I mean. Bringing one lassie by herself.'

Rosamond was laughing helplessly. 'I told him the other day I found MacQueen's very happy-go-lucky behind the scenes ... I've never had a job like this before. I don't know what to make of it.'

Goldie was surely an original. 'Take it as it comes. You'll find we all go along with what Gaspard wants. He wrote and told me you were someone special, and that I must get to know you. What did he mean, particularly? I made up my mind I'd ask straight out. Or have I gone too far?'

Rosamond cast a quick, appealing glance at Matthieu, but he was no help to her; he leaned back in his chair and said, lines of laughter creasing his cheeks, 'It's a wonder you didn't leap to the wrong conclusions as I did, at our first encounter. I thought the old boy had

gone off his rocker and fallen for a girl young enough
to be his own granddaughter.'

Humphrey and Goldie looked staggered. She said,
'You thought *what*? About Gaspard? You ought to be
whipped!'

Rosamond thought she ought to get in. 'Instead of
which, Mrs Humphrey, Gaspard was looking on me as
someone who might in very truth have been his granddaughter. Gaspard had very tender feelings for my
grandmother long ago, before he married Ellie, but they
quarrelled and parted and she went to England and
married someone else. He knew the moment he saw me
that I must be her descendant, and my name confirmed
it.'

Goldie said quickly, 'Was she Rosamond too?'

Rosamond shook her head. 'Her second name was.
Louise Rosamond.'

The meal over, Goldie and Rosamond were banished
from the kitchen while the men did the dishes. 'Little
enough return for a meal like that,' said Matthieu.

As Rosamond wandered round Goldie's pot-plants in
the wing of the house that was their own, her mind
harked back to what Verna had said. Matthieu selfish?
No, here he was, washing up.

Goldie said, 'Gaspard knows so well a woman and
her man must have a corner they can call their very
own. So he had this altered years ago so it can be shut
off from the other if we want it that way. Also, he can
entertain entirely on his own if he finds it suits him, or
his guests. If the farm family come up, I just leave them
to it. In the light of what's happening, you ought to
know that. If ever another woman is mistress here, it
would be completely her domain. I'd just be through
that door if I was needed.'

Rosamond caught her breath in. What did one reply
to that? Goldie had jumped to her own conclusions. Or
were they her own? Had Gaspard put them into her
head in letters? It was obvious this family had a tradi-

tion of early marriages. They'd like to see the only bachelor settled down.

Was it true Pierre had married to please Gaspard? Was the old man still rather tyrannical at heart? Lovingly so, but still pulling the strings? She could imagine Gaspard, carried away by meeting the granddaughter of the woman he loved, planning a marriage. Matthieu heard regularly from Gaspard, she knew.

She didn't know how to answer, so she didn't. She had a feeling Goldie didn't really expect one. She'd stated a fact, cleared the ground, in case this girl wondered.

Rosamond went on admiring the trailing creepers, the luxuriant growth of the maidenhair ferns, remarked that the plants she'd always called Busy Lizzies back home, were called water fuchsias here. Goldie seemed satisfied. They came back to the house, had the coffee and biscuits the men had ready.

Goldie suggested Matthieu should show Rosamond the rest of the house. As they left the room, she called after them, 'I think you'd find it interesting to look at the fly-leaves of the books on the headboard of his bed.'

As they mounted the stairs, Matthieu said, 'What bee has she got in her bonnet now?'

'I've no idea, but it would be interesting to find out.'

As they entered the big room at the corner of the house, so that it looked north and west, Rosamond gave a cry of delight. 'This is lovely! What character, for a bedroom.'

Matthieu said thoughtfully, 'In my grandmother's day it was a very conventional bedroom, all frilled satin and valances. But gradually Grandfather brought the books in—said he liked to wake up in the night or the morning to find his treasures all about him. He's a great reader. He's also rather a poetic old beggar, you know, and rather vulnerable, despite that hard crust. Not that you'd know about that, you got under it from the start.'

'Yes, but that was simply and solely because I looked like my grandmother.'

Curved shelves had been set into the walls here and there, with some choice ornaments from that exquisite department at the store on the top shelves, the rest crowded with books old and new.

Rosamond fingered them appreciatively. Some were so loved they were shabby with re-reading, others bright and shiny in their book covers, evidence of a mind that despite its years was not static.

They were drawn to the bedhead. It had been specially designed to hold two rows of books. There was his Bible, his hymn book, some volumes of poetry, Tennyson, Wordsworth, Burns, Browning, a couple of anthologies. They opened these at the fly-leaves. They had Gaspard's name written in them, no more. One had 'Margot Somers' written in a firm clear hand. She had known and loved these verses when she was young. Matthieu picked up another, a school anthology of verse, *Mount Helicon.* A memory stirred in Rosamond's mind. 'I wonder. When my grandparents went to Canada, Gran gave me her copy of this. I distinctly remember the fly-leaf was torn out. One poem was underlined and someone, not Gran because it wasn't her writing, had written under it, "Yes." It intrigued me. I asked her straight out who had written it, and she laughed mischievously and said, 'Some things, dear child, are not for one's descendants to know.'

Matthieu opened this copy. He shifted the book to his left hand, put his right arm about Rosamond's shoulders, and moved to the window with her. They gazed down at the inscription. 'For Gaspard from Louise. See the Sonnet on page 14.' Rosamond turned the pages for him. Three lines of the fourteen were underlined:

'Let me not to the marriage of true minds
Admit impediments. Love is not love
Which alters when it alteration finds . . .'

Matthieu said, 'Which poem in yours was underlined, Rosamond? Could you remember?'

'One of Burns. I'll find it in the index.' She did. They read:

> 'O my Luve's like a red, red rose
> That's newly sprung in June;
> O my Luve's like the melodie
> That's sweetly played in tune.'

She repeated the words. Their eyes fell to the last verse. Matthieu read it aloud:

> ' "And fare thee weel, my only Luve!
> And fare thee weel awhile!
> And I will come again, my Luve,
> Tho' it were ten thousand mile." '

The pathos of it caught at them. Matthieu said, 'It was more than ten thousand miles that stretched between them. Thirteen thousand, in fact. But now ... Grandfather will be back soon. Whereabouts in Canada is your grandmother, Rosamond?'

'Vancouver.'

'Vancouver ... um ... seven thousand miles, roughly. Not as far as it used to be, in more ways than one. Better and better. Girl, if Fate is reluctant to bring about a meeting between these two I think we should nudge her elbow a bit, don't you?' He looked down on her. 'What are you looking like that for? Are you one who thinks of love as just something that happens to the young? Springtime romance, not autumn? Shame on you!'

She shook her head. 'No, I've seen too many happy late-in-life marriages, ones at which my father officiated. It's immature to think that way, and I don't think I'm that.'

'I don't think you are either. You're very mature. In fact sometimes I'd like you to be a little more uninhibited, to let yourself go. I think that fellow Jeffrey checked something in you. I'm making no apologies for bringing his name up. Better you should realise he wasn't worth a tin of fish than have you just about pass out at the sight of him.'

An angry red stained her cheekbones. 'I felt nothing for him at all. He was the last straw in a very tense day. I'm not in the least inhibited, you know I'm not. You said once I was a funny girl the way I'd suddenly flare up. That's not being inhibited.'

'Oh, I know you can fly off the handle. Praise be you can. Anybody who couldn't would never do me. I don't mean you're placid in temper. I mean you don't let yourself go in other directions. Jeffrey made you very cautious. You're afraid to trust your own judgment with men, particularly with me.'

'Perhaps you've got something there. I wouldn't let my heart rule my head again. If I'd not been swept off my feet then, I could have read the signs. It couldn't have lasted—nothing of the marriage of true minds there. I'd have been bored to tears within a year. I had a lucky escape.'

'So next time you're going to weigh up the pros and cons. That it?'

'Yes, and if it sounds cold-blooded, I can't help it. I think sweet reason has to be brought to bear upon choosing a marriage partner.'

Surprisingly, Matthieu agreed. 'Yes, it does. Pierre fell madly in love, but it fizzled out in three months, thank goodness. The second time round he couldn't have done better.'

Her brows drew together. 'In whose opinion? Your grandfather's? Did he call the tune and pay the piper?'

'Nothing of the kind. Pierre picked Natalie himself. Although——'

'Although what? You can't stop there.'

He said slowly, 'I'd hate you to think anything less of Grandfather because of it. But I don't want you to think that Grandfather acted the tyrant.' He started to laugh. 'It was little less than magnificent. The first one was a real gold-digger. Mum and Dad were away, and Grandfather *in loco parentis*. Just as well, but the old man took a frightful risk. He made up to the girl himself, and she dropped Pierre like a hot potato. Grandfather extricated himself very neatly, Pierre's eyes were opened . . . Natalie happened along at the psychological moment . . . and that's as near a match made in heaven as you could get. What do you think of that?'

Rosamond regarded him steadily. 'I'm not at all sure what I think of it. Without knowing the main characters and actually seeing it happen, I couldn't presume to judge. I don't know the girl. I hope she didn't get too hurt.'

His mouth was wry as if he wished he'd not told her. 'She was like Verna, if you want to know, but without her redeeming features. Self-seeking to the core.'

She said slowly, 'Your grandfather said there was a hard streak in all the MacQueen men, and I'm beginning to believe it.'

He took the book from her, looked down on it. 'I'd have thought this was proof we aren't. Grandfather was heading that way, but changed. I thought by the very fact you know I'm sentimental about my grandfather and his Louise you'd realise I'm not hard. In me, the tough old pioneer streak is watered down, especially by my mother's blood. You'd love her. You and she are two of a kind.'

The thought raced through her mind: But what of your grandmother's blood? That mischief-maker. The cold, implacable woman.

He gave Rosamond a little shake. 'I got off on the wrong foot with you, and I think you still hold that against me. I can't wipe it out, but you still don't have too fixed an idea about that, do you? You don't think I still have my doubts about that weekend? Because I don't.'

She looked up at him searchingly. 'Are you sure? I couldn't stand it if you had even a vestige of doubt left.'

The tawny eyes looked steadily into hers and there wasn't a trace of laughter left in them. 'I *know* there was nothing in it. As I've come to know you, I've realised you're a marriage-or-nothing girl. Satisfied? You'd better be, because I can't go on protesting I've no doubts left. It would sound phoney. *Are you satisfied?*'

Her slow smile began, her mouth softened, curved. A dimple appeared. Matthieu didn't respond immediately, but kept holding her gaze. Then he smiled too. 'You muggins! You must know how I feel about you. I——'

She put her hand over his lips, but was smiling. 'Matthieu, you go too fast! Give me time for . . .'

'For sweet reason to bear upon the situation?' His eyes mocked.

'It's what I want,' she said firmly. 'I was swept off my feet once, but never again. Let's play it cool.'

He gave her an incredulous look. 'Play it cool? To hell with that! We'll play it my way, and that's like this!'

The way he kissed her certainly wasn't cool. Neither was the way she responded. When at last he released her he was laughing. 'See . . . you're not capable of playing it cool either! But I'll hold my tongue. Perhaps I *am* rushing my fences. *And* rushing Grandfather's. But in his case, waiting too long would be unthinkable. Time is running out for two people called Gaspard and Louise. Give me your grandmother's address. I'll send it to Grandfather and tell him she's a widow. He might come home via Canada.'

She said, 'Not yet, please. I must find out first, somehow, without giving things away, if she too has ever looked back with longing. It could so easily have been someone else my grandmother loved and lost. Oh, I don't doubt there was something between her and Gaspard, but I'm almost sure it was only a passing fancy.'

Into his frustrated silence came the sound of Goldie's voice, calling him to the telephone.

CHAPTER SEVEN

WHEN Matthieu came back he said, 'You've got yourself a respite. That was my travel agent, my bookings for

Australia are through. I'm only sorry it's coming before Grandfather is back, though he said I was to go just the same. I'm on a committee dealing with Inter-Tasman Reciprocal Trade ... the old man's very keen on this, naturally. I am myself, but I wish I'd not had to go with both him and Pierre away. However, that's the way of it. I leave next Wednesday. I'd be glad if it made you miss me.'

Rosamond knew she'd be glad of the respite. Had it not been for what Verna had said she wouldn't have had all these doubts and fears. But she would be unwise to dismiss them. She could well imagine Gaspard nudging his nephew towards marriage to Louise's descendant. She knew how frequently Gaspard wrote his grandson. Matthieu had said one day, 'He's always been a good correspondent, but he's getting prolific—something to do with you, I suspect. He wants to know every last detail about how you're settling in and am I making you feel at home.'

Matthieu walked her home. He got her autumn jacket from the guest-room where she'd laid it, a green, edged with soft beige fur at the cuffs and round the hood she hardly ever pulled up. But he pulled it up now. 'There's a tinge of frost in the air tonight. The true autumn is nearly here. April is the month for the golds and russets.' He tied the cord at her neck. It was decorated with twin fur bobbles. He put his hands inside the hood, drew a tendril of hair out each side, adjusted the hood till it was perfectly symmetrical. His touch was doing things to her. To cover that awareness she said breathlessly, 'A draper to the nth degree ... everything must be perfect!'

He laughed spontaneously and said, 'That's what *you* think.'

Rosamond wrinkled her nose. 'What do you mean? That you're not a perfectionist?'

'No, I meant something different, but I'm not ready to tell you yet. I will when I come back from Australia.

But I wasn't striving for perfection then, I just wanted to touch you. But I won't go into that—you want time. Anyway, before we go any further, there's something you must know. But I don't want to tell you just before I go away.'

'What can you mean? Tell me now! You've got me wondering.'

Matthieu was adamant. 'No, if you can have your reserves, I can have mine. You've adjusted to a lot in a short time. I'll take it a step at a time. You told me not to rush my fences. Come on—Goldie said I was to give you those lemmingtons you liked with the cream and slices of Kiwi fruit on top. I'll just get them.'

While he was in the kitchen the phone rang and he called out to Rosamond to answer it. She recognised the voice immediately: Verna's mother. Unfortunately the recognition was mutual. Mrs Halley said, 'Oh, is that you, Rosamond?'

She had a wild desire to mutter, 'Wrong number,' and hang up, but resisted it. She said casually, 'Oh, do you want Mr Matthieu? He's with Mrs Humphrey at the moment. I'm just leaving. I'll get him.'

She was aware Matthieu was glad he could offer Australia as an excuse not to accept an invitation. He answered questions about his grandfather: 'Not much point in writing at the moment, I'm afraid. Your letter would chase him all round the world, and he'd probably not get it till he got back here. Every letter is from a different country. The old boy's living it up, he might even go to Canada on the way home. I've got my suspicions about that ... he spent some time there on his way. I've a feeling he might even bring a bride back with him. No, I'm serious. Well, I must get Rosamond home now. I'll see you when I get back. Goodbye for now.'

There was sparkle about the evening. It was full of moonlight and tree-shadows and they went home by way of Carlton Mill Bridge.

Rosamond said, 'Matthieu, was that wise . . . to tease Mrs Halley that your grandfather might come back with a bride?'

He chuckled, quite unrepentant. 'I couldn't resist it. What matter?'

She was conscious of the magic of that night, the moon silvering the trees that bordered the sweetly-flowing Avon, the enchantment of walking step by step with someone so kindred, someone whose forebear's life had touched so intimately her forebear's, but some innate caution made her keep their farewell brief. He insisted he turn her lights on, take a reassuring look around to see all was well. 'I don't like you living alone.'

Then he drew her out on to the terrace where the Virginia creeper was just beginning to turn red. 'Neither do I like leaving you.' He sensed her instant withdrawal, and laughed. 'I'm not making a bid to stay, goose. I know, by now, your standards.'

Rosamond was moved to delicious laughter. 'Oh, Matthieu, when I first saw your furious face, looking down on me, how could I ever have thought I'd live to hear you utter words like that?'

He laughed too, drawing her back.

She said, 'But I was hardly less furious, myself. I was mad clean through. I was glad Gaspard hadn't seen you. I couldn't have borne it for him if his happy weekend had been overlaid with such a beastly suspicion. To me he was just an old man, looking back on a youthful attachment.'

He nodded. 'Time was when Pierre and I thought of him that way, till he successfully drew off that gold-digger girl. It was hilarious in some moments, but we did see him in a new light . . . as a man, not a grand-father.'

'Why are you telling me these things, Matthieu?' she asked.

'Because I feel that even though we've become such—become so close so soon—you still hold out on me. You

say it's not that you still carry scars because Jeffrey let
you down, so I feel it's a hangover from the way we
first met.'

'It isn't either of those things. It's just canniness.
Matthieu, it's time you went home.'

He kissed her briefly and quoted, ' "Parting is such
sweet sorrow that I could say goodnight till it be
morrow." What *are* you laughing at now? You could
make me selfconscious!'

'I'm sorry, Matthieu. I've a very awkward subconsci-
ous. It presents me with nearly forgotten things at the
most embarrassing moments. It used to irritate Jeff
beyond belief, but it wouldn't you, I think. I remembered Dad telling a joke at a wedding breakfast.
About the father upstairs who thought his daughter's
fiancé would never go home. Finally the young man
quoted that and the father, leaning over the banisters
said, "Well, just wait sixty seconds, young man, and it
will be tomorrow." '

He said, mock-seriously, 'I don't know I feel any
better than Jeff. You spoiled my exit line. You were
meant to think about me romantically when I'd gone
because I'd actually quoted poetry. I'm going to be flat
out now till I leave for overseas. I'll have to get out
sheaves of papers, statistics, prepare a speech, get them
typed. And soon after I get back we'll have all the hoo-
ha of Grandfather and Pierre and Natalie arriving, and
our idyllic evenings will get overlaid. And you and I will
have things to discuss, quite seriously. No, don't ask me
what. I'm playing tit-for-tat. I'm waiting for the time
and the place.'

He didn't kiss her again, he squeezed her fingers,
walked away.

Rosamond lay a long time savouring the happenings
of the evening. Some things were puzzling, some promised her a happy future, she thought. What a strange
family they were! That bizarre story of Gaspard playing
up to the little gold-digger. Of course a lot of money
was involved in a business the size of theirs. Girls were

lucky who met and fell in love with someone whose circumstances equalled their own, who knew the joy of working together to buy a modest home for themselves, knew no one could suspect them of feathering a nest.

Life in the office moved at a terrific pace on the Friday, the Monday, the Tuesday. On the Monday Rosamond was amazed to get a toll-call from Jeffrey, from Queenstown. She sounded a cautious note. 'Jeffrey, I'm frightfully busy. Mr Matthieu's off to Australia in two days' time and we're putting through as much stuff as possible for the ads before he goes, so——'

Jeffrey was always hard to slap down. 'I think you're quite a favoured member of the staff. I'm sure he'll not begrudge you a few moments. I wanted to tell you what a fantastically successful tourist conference this has been, and also that something's cropped up in which you could be interested, seeing your parents are in Dunedin. That's the doorstep to this Central Otago paradise ... you'd love it. I'm negotiating for property here. There are several to choose from. If I can get them for the right price. . . .'

He went on. She was aware someone had come in behind her, glanced back to see Matthieu, said to Jeffrey, 'Just a moment, please,' and without bothering to put her hand over the mouthpiece, said, 'I won't be long. Sorry about this,' then into the phone, 'I'm needed by Mr Matthieu. Well, I'll wish you well, Jeffrey, but it's nothing to do with me. No, I don't think I'll be that way for ages. You don't start thinking about holidays when you've just got settled in a new job. I've had a weekend with Mother and Dad. The next visit will be from them to me. Now, goodbye.'

She put the phone down and glared at it. 'Conceited hound! He can't believe that now I'm free he can't take up where we left off. He's thinking about buying motels in Queenstown. I wish to goodness he'd be content with the complex in Auckland. Sorry to keep you waiting. Is there something you want me to do?'

'Yes, I'd like you to come across to both papers immediately. This,' tapping some cuttings, 'needs discussion.' They hurried out. He said, as they drove, 'You know how to cut the knot, don't you? Don't keep a fellow dangling as a sort of second string to one's fiddle, like girls do.'

She giggled. 'Dangling strings wouldn't produce much music, my dear boss. You're mixing your metaphors.'

'Could it be you know your future holds a very different life from that?'

'Well, it certainly doesn't hold Jeff Vane. That's enough for now.'

He patted her knee. 'Fair enough, here we are.' They got out after much difficult parking, and Matthieu gazed round them. 'City traffic, city noises ... and in Central Otago where Jeffrey Vane is right now, the rams are out with the ewes and most of the snow is gone from the high tops ... and the lake will be sapphire blue ... and they'll be burning off stubble, the air will be full of the tang of it. And the riverbeds and hills will be bright with poplars and willows ... and I've got to cross the Tasman and get involved in hours of discussion! There'll be tobacco smoke tainting the air inside and petrol reek outside, like here. I wouldn't mind if I was getting away into their outback ... oh, well, it's got to be done.'

There had been sheer nostalgia in his voice. These MacQueens were strange men. Generations of Scots farmers lay behind them, plus years of establishing a fine business, and they seemed never to be entirely satisfied with city life.

On Tuesday Rosamond knew a weight of the spirit that was almost unbearable. The next ten days were stretching out in front of her like an arid desert, days when she wouldn't even catch a glimpse of him dashing from department to department, admiring or criticising displays, serving the odd customer and never reckoning it beneath his dignity, smoothing down complaining customers, inspiring salespeople with his own enthusiasm.

She wished, oh, how she wished she'd been in a more surrendering mood the other night. If she'd let him declare himself, how sweet it would have been now. Yet ... oh, it was too soon. She was wise to have delayed things. But she would be glad beyond measure when he came back.

There was a big sheaf of ads that needed his signature, and she went along to his offices with them. Shona, Matthieu's secretary, looked up and smiled a⁺ her. 'He's on the phone. Like to wait? Right. I'm typing his speech, the final draft, I hope. We've got miles of other letters to get through after this.' Her house phone rang. Hanging up, she said, 'Just my luck! The accountant wants me. Rosamond, this is straight copying. Be a darling and finish it off ... just one page. You will? Thanks a million.'

Rosamond said, 'I'll just leave these ads when I finish. I can see you're in a tizz. Would you get him to sign them? The fewer interruptions he has the better. Be sure to check what I type, won't you?'

The content surprised her with its technicality ... far more like a farming treatise than drapery. Well, wool was the basic thing, of course. It was interesting, though she wished she'd read the introduction and the body of it. She finished it, looked over what she'd typed, in case of errors.

Into the silence fell Matthieu's voice. He chuckled, 'Yes, we sure do have fun as a family protecting our financial interests. Oh, yes, she's undoubtedly on the make, biding her time till Grandfather gets back. No, of course not, I'm too wily a bird to be taken in. Of course I can handle it. No, I'm not telling you the details on the phone—don't forget we have a switchboard. No, he'll never wake up some morning to find himself married to her. He's too shrewd. Remember how he saved Pierre from making a fool of himself? Now the younger generation does it in reverse! That's all I can say. I must go. Love to everyone. What did you say? Yes, I will. . . .' But before he had uttered that final goodbye, Rosamond had gone. That was too private a conversation to be overheard . . . and if he had come out, she couldn't help but give it away that she had heard. There was something in it she didn't like, something that threatened her peace of mind . . . she had to have time to sort it out. She fled.

She was glad nothing had brought him to her office. She raced through her work, trying to shut out what she'd heard, and when failing in that, trying to apply it to what knowledge she'd gained of the family.

At five-twenty-five she realised she might be able to get away without seeing him, even to say goodbye. At two minutes before the half-hour Shona appeared, 'Thanks for the typing, it helped us get through. I'm staying on for a quarter of an hour. Mr Matthieu said would you wait till quarter to six and he'll run you home then.'

Shona had a half-smile at the back of her eyes. She was well aware there was more than an employer–employee relationship between them. Rosamond had her bag ready on her desk. 'Sorry, but I've an appointment. I'm having dinner out and I'm being picked up. Traffic's dense at this hour and he can't stop for more than a moment outside the staff door. I'm sure all my work is up to date. Thanks a lot, Shona, tell him I hope he has a successful trip,' and she whirled out of the door as if indeed she hadn't a moment to lose. She was quite surprised at her powers of invention.

She stepped straight into a convenient taxi and drove out to a suburban restaurant Barbara had once taken her to. She didn't want to risk having Matthieu ring or call. She went to a cinema afterwards, had coffee and a doughnut at a snack bar after that, then took another taxi home. It was past midnight. He'd have given her up long since, because he was leaving practically the crack of dawn.

The moment she got into bed her postponed thoughts

rose up and jeered at her. All the unease she'd felt when
she'd heard that telephone conversation surged over
her. Against her wild desire for it to be as ambiguous as
what Matthieu had heard his grandfather say in Southampton was the inner conviction that it was *everything*
to do with *her*.

Now she made herself analyse that conviction. The
memory of the way Gaspard had interfered to save
Pierre from an unsuitable marriage rose up and gib-
bered at her. Spell it out, Rosamond. Don't be afraid
to, my girl. Gaspard had pretended to fall for the girl
himself; now Matthieu was doing it in reverse. Face it,
he never had believed her explanation of what Gaspard
had said about that weekend. What an actor he must
be! He had certainly fooled her. He'd even, with great
cunning, pretended he'd like to bring Louise and Gaspard together. That would be in case she began to suspect what he was doing. But his own overheard conversation had given him away completely. Who on earth
could he have been talking to? It had sounded like
family. Well, didn't he have a sister on a farm somewhere? But what did that matter? The thing was, he
must never know she'd overheard.

What a gullible fool she'd been! She'd known a rush
of warmth towards him when he'd said he thought she
was a marriage-or-nothing sort of girl. He'd had his
tongue in his cheek, for sure . . . meaning that only marriage could secure her a financial interest in the business. An old man's darling! A scalding pity for old Gaspard touched her heart. Disillusioned in his wife long
ago and now deceived so unnecessarily by his grandson.
And what she, Rosamond, must do would hurt Gaspard too. Only there was nothing else she *could* do. She
was going to cut and run, otherwise Matthieu would
watch her like a hawk. Every gesture of affection she
made towards the old man would be suspect. She would
fade out of their lives completely, and now was the
time, the ideal time to do it.

Her mind worked rapidly. The flat was leased to the

firm, not to her. She could just walk out of it. She'd go down to her parents for a break, then decide what to do. It could be possible to take up her interrupted studies. Dad would know. She still had plenty of money left from the sale of her car, plus her savings. She might even, if living at home, be able to get part-time work while taking lectures. She could now, at least, please herself. And now she would sleep. She wasn't going to make herself ill from loss of sleep, worrying over a man as calculating as Matthieu MacQueen. She just wished she could see his face when he returned from Australia to find her gone. She fell forty fathoms deep into slumber from which she was only roused by the ringing of her telephone.

She fell out of bed, staggered out to the living-room, and snatched it up. Matthieu!

He said, 'Oh, you *are* there! I rang half an hour ago and there was no answer. Surely you don't sleep as soundly as that? Are you all right, Rosamond? I was worried.'

'Of course I'm all right. I don't think I've ever slept through a telephone ringing before, but I was very late last night. But perhaps you rang the wrong number.' She peered at her watch, 'I say, you ought to be at the airport. The flight's not cancelled, is it?'

'I *am* at the airport—took one last chance. Where did you get to last night? Shona said you were out to dinner. You didn't tell me that earlier.'

'No reason to, dear man. I knew you were busy. And we were, as I said, late.'

'I know that. I rang till quarter to twelve, then decided I'd better have some sleep myself.'

He sounded really disgruntled. Rosamond was glad about that. Very.

He continued, 'Who were you out with?' As if he had the right.

She said sweetly, 'You wouldn't know him. No one from the shop. We saw a very good comedy. Pity you can't see it.'

A silence. 'How did you get to know this fellow?'

She didn't hesitate. 'He's the brother of one of the girls at the library. I've become friendly with her, and visited their home recently.' True enough, except that there'd been no brother.

'Oh, well, watch your step while I'm away. I don't like——'

She cut in, 'Matthieu, it must be perilously near your embarking time, I can hear the inter-com. Don't miss it. Is it your call?'

'It is, dammit. This is most unsatisfactory. I'll just have to say goodbye, Rosamond, and——'

'Goodbye, Matthieu,' she said, and replaced the phone. There hadn't been a tremor in her voice, but now she stood leaning against the wall, tears pouring down her cheeks.

She was proud of the way she managed to concentrate on her work. It was a relief that Matthieu wasn't there. No having to steal herself against the disturbing charm of his presence. Oddly, though she'd expected it to be a day when nothing would go right, everything went on oiled wheels. Good, she would leave everything up to date. She would give in a week's notice soon. That would be adequate. This was a created position. They would just move the girl next to Monica up one when she married, and get a new bottom-runger. She'd give herself two days to settle her mind, convince herself she wasn't acting irresponsibly.

The whole situation had been highly emotional from start to finish, triggered off by her connections with Gaspard's sentimental past. If she herself wasn't deeply involved in her own feelings, none of it would have mattered. But she couldn't cause herself the anguish of staying on, loving Matthieu, yet knowing how devious he was.

It was late afternoon when she called at Shona's office for the ads he would have okayed. They hadn't been sent back. Shona was flat out. 'He left them on his desk for you, and said there were also some ad clippings you'd want filed. We got them from your filing clerk yesterday when you were at lunch. Just check they're all there. His desk isn't as tidy as usual.'

Rosamond went in, found most of the clippings on top, found some were missing, shuffled through a mound of papers and found them. There was also one roughly torn out, a nondescript piece of newsprint. She examined it more carefully. It was about half a sheet and had a big blue pencil mark round a section of a couple of columns. Oh, there were tiny scatter ads in the miscellaneous column. She'd wondered that a firm this size bothered with them, but Matthieu had assured her they really paid off. She'd better file them. He wouldn't have torn them out if he hadn't wanted them.

Back in her office she was sorting them when her eye fell on one in the left column. *Situations Vacant.*

> 'Wanted: Governess for remote lakeside sheep-station in Central Otago. Not a qualified teacher but one able to keep discipline and supervise correspondence lessons for two children aged six and eight. Apply in person to Mrs Logan MacCorquodale, United Service Hotel, Cathedral Square, between the hours of 2 and 4 on Thursday and Friday, the 22nd and 23rd. Definite appointment can be made by telephone. An excellent wage would be given to compensate for lack of easy access to city amenities.'

Rosamond became almost transfixed staring at it. Central Otago; Dunedin was the doorstep to that area. Not too far from her people. She'd heard it was a glorious scenic area . . . fancy living on the shores of a lake. She wondered which one. She mightn't have much chance of securing the position, but she'd give it a jolly good try. The desolation of her heart began to ease. Here was something definite to attempt. The thought of escape was wonderful to contemplate.

She was quite glad to see Verna coming up her path that night. Much healthier to have company than to be

alone with one's churning thoughts. Verna was fun,
scatty but amusing. It was much later in the night that
Verna said, 'I rang you last night but couldn't get you. I
guessed you'd be out with Matthieu, a farewell dinner
or something?'

Rosamond opened her eyes wide, gave a credible
imitation of surprise, said, 'Good heavens, no, I was
out with someone else, dinner, cinema, etc. I didn't get
in till midnight. I took your warning seriously, you
know. I think the MacQueens are a funny lot. I'd rather
keep relations with them strictly business. I never did
like being too friendly with the management. I think
Matthieu has an idea, much exaggerated, of his own
and his grandfather's eligibility, and I'd loathe the
thought that any man thought I was the sort to marry
for money, or even where money is.'

'Good for you! You know, after I spoke to you I felt
a bit foolish, wondered if it had been wise. You know
how it is . . . if anyone warns you against a person, you
feel like flying to their defence. And Matthieu *can* be
charming if it suits his book. All the MacQueens have
the idea you just mentioned, that they're the targets of
fortune-hunters. He got a scare when he went overseas,
thought old Gaspard was falling for someone quite
young. He said he had visions of having to stay to ex-
tricate him . . . by making up to her himself and then
leaving her cold. But Grandpapa went off quite happily
to Russia and the girl faded out. Mum told Matthieu
he'd probably find Gaspard in tow with a ballerina
next. Shows how much notice she took of Matthieu!'

It was lightly said, but Rosamond found her hands
were clenched and said lightly, in turn, 'Bless my boots,
what utter vanity! Well, he'll come a thud himself some
day. I could easily have imagined him a different sort of
man. I suppose I got all carried away with him rescuing
me from Jeff that day.' An idea struck her. She gave a
smile she hoped might be taken for a tenderly remini-
scent one. 'In any case, I'm sorry now he did rescue me.'

Verna looked really astonished. 'Why?'

'I think I misjudged Jeff. At the time we broke our engagement he probably felt I didn't love him enough, that I was putting my family before him. As I was, I'll admit, only their need was greater than his. Anyway, we've been in touch again. He rang me from Queenstown. He's thinking of buying motels in Queenstown. He baited the hook by saying my people were, after all, in Otago. I may just go south, anyway. Nothing really to keep me in Christchurch.'

Verna nodded. 'I see your point. So you may look for an opening down there. I should think one of the firms there would leap at you. Look, what am I talking like this for? I'd miss you horribly.'

'But you could come down and stay with us, see how the other half of the world lives. Manse life isn't like yours, but it's fun.'

When Verna had gone Rosamond felt she'd paved the way for her flitting. It wasn't likely she'd get this governess job, but it would make no difference ... before Matthieu MacQueen was back in New Zealand, she would be gone.

She got an appointment, went to Don Yelland and asked if she might have an hour off. She felt a heel when he told her to take the rest of the afternoon. 'Matthieu told me you'd worked flat out on the ads before he left, so I guess you've earned a break. And don't come back for late shopping night. I won't expect you till Monday.'

Mrs Logan MacCorquodale had, for some reason, sounded like a sonsy matron. Instead she was tall, slim, with copper hair and bluey-green eyes and only a year or two older than Rosamond. Added to that, her voice sounded decidedly English, but not so. 'I was born in New Zealand, but my mother was English and after we lost Dad she took me back there. Not right away, because she did governessing on the lake too, but now she's remarried and so we all live at Glen Airlie in Central Otago, not far from Arrowtown, on Lake Moana-

Kotare. In England we lived near Haslemere in Surrey. Where did you?'

'My father was a minister, so we moved around, but the last few years I've been in Southampton. I should say I began to train for teaching or lecturing, but my father got crippled, so I went into advertising. I've got my references here. Dad made a complete recovery and came out to a Dunedin parish. I decided to follow them. I've had a look round here, but I'd rather be down south.

'I rang up the Education Board when I saw your advertisement and they were able to tell me how this correspondence school works. They said that as so many mothers have to manage lessons as well as housekeeping, I should be able to manage. So I thought I'd apply. Of course you may have others more qualified, but anyway, what's involved at Glen Airlie? ... Have you really got children six and eight? You look far too young. Or are they workers' children?'

Elissa MacCorquodale laughed. 'No, I'm just doing the interviewing for the next station uplake. I've only one small son, James, the light of our lives and the bane of our existence. But Logan and I are having a break. He's at a conference, and my mother is looking after James. Now before we go into more details, I must tell you that although we have an access road at Glen Airlie, they don't at Strathdearn. Actually, the road has reached Glen Airlie only the last few years. So what you're applying for has access by water only, from Ludwigtown, across the lake.

'I went to High School there when my mother was governess at Glen Airlie, so I know a fair bit about it, because then we only reached there by launch. So you might miss civilisation. We have to create our own pattern of living on these big remote sheep-stations, and if you're used to Southampton, it could be too much for you. It's different when you're married ... great compensations. Mind you, we go across to Ludwigtown a lot, and we're always having tourists drop in. It's differ-

ent now from in the past when they had to rely on a
fortnightly launch service for mail and supplies. But
Strathdearn, like Glen Airlie, has its own launch, plus a
miniature fleet of small boats.'

Rosamond couldn't keep the sparkle from her eyes.
'I'm very mechanically minded for a girl. I love messing
about with boats. When you live on the edge of the
Solent, you seem to get boat-minded. I'm not so keen
on yachting, but I love a boat engine.'

Elissa gained a matching sparkle. 'I think you could
be just what I'm looking for, for Emilie. I'd better explain the set-up, see how you fancy it. Emilie's husband
is Rodney MacGilpin. They have two girls, Fanny eight
and Helene six. Geordie, their only son, is just a toddler.
They have quite a staff, housed in quarters, with an old
man, a pet, who cooks for them. The schoolroom is
over in the old homestead where you would sleep. The
Macks look after that, and the brother. He's a bachelor.
But at present he's away, so the Macks are in Akaroa
on holiday. You'd stay in the new house just now.'

'If I get the job,' said Rosamond.

'You've got it. I feel it in my bones you're going to be
right for it. You've got the know-how, you can handle a
boat, and you're a minister's daughter. Poor Emilie,
she's managed it herself this term and it was getting her
down, because Geordie's a handful at his age. But the
governess they had last year turned out to be an alco-
holic—distressing, but it meant they couldn't leave the
children alone with her. They were good, made arrangements for her to have treatment, and Emilie struggled
on alone. Now, as you aren't in a job, having so recently come from England, you could start pretty soon,
I suppose? We'd like to have the children settled with
someone before Easter, and this year the May term
holidays come so soon after that.'

Rosamond made up her mind. 'I could start a week
come Tuesday. What arrangements could be made for
getting me across the lake? I can easily make my way to
Ludwigtown.' It was as easy as that.

Events moved so fast Rosamond had no time for regrets. Mr Yelland was astounded and dismayed. 'You mean you're giving up this job and going down to your parents just to look round for something similar? It won't be easy to get anything comparable. I thought with Mr MacQueen bringing you out here that this would have been a permanent position.'

'I think you know I wouldn't let him pay my fare, though he did treat me to the accommodation. I felt I'd feel freer if there were no strings attached to the job. Don't feel too badly ... I may not even go to another firm. I may, if possible, take up studies again.'

The accountant hesitated, made up his mind, and plunged. 'I thought this wasn't just a business arrangement, that there was something more personal in it than that. And also ...' he hesitated again, then, 'apart from the personal angle Mr MacQueen hinted at in his letter to me, I thought there was a growing attachment between you and Mr Matthieu. Sorry to make this point, but if, say, you've quarrelled, Rosamond, I do beg you to wait till he gets back from this mission to Canberra. I feel he'll be very angry with me for letting you go. He's a good lad, and I'd hate to see him upset.'

Rosamond said, 'Mr Yelland, you've been sweet. I know you didn't find that easy to say. I'd better be honest. It *is* more for personal reasons that I'm leaving. If this could have remained purely a business appointment I wouldn't have dreamed of leaving. I told Mr Matthieu from the start I didn't think it was wise to mix personal feelings and business life, but he wouldn't let it stay that way. I'll leave him a note, tell him why I'm leaving. There'll be no comeback as far as you're concerned. Nobody could stop me. I'm glad he's not here, I don't want any unpleasantness. May I ask a favour of you?' she added. 'Would you keep this confidential till Friday? I'll be leaving then and setting off for Dunedin on Saturday. I'm not even telling Mrs Berridge till then, or the girls in my section. It will be the neatest way of flitting. To them I'll just say I want to be with my people, and that I wanted no fuss made because I've been here so short a time.'

He was unhappy, but had to take it. Rosamond decided to say no more to her parents than that she'd be coming for the weekend. Once there she could explain as much or as little to them as she wished.

Thelma, told on Friday morning, was horrified, took Rosamond into her buying-office and tried to persuade her to at least wait till Matthieu was home. It was hard to keep it to a business footing. In the end Thelma said flatly, 'I think this is completely out of character as far as you're concerned. I don't think it's a desire to go home to live, or to see if you can take up studies again. I think you and Matthieu have quarrelled. Haven't you heard the course of true love never runs smoothly? But it's absurd to cut and run, it doesn't give the troubled waters a chance to subside! I don't care if Don Yelland *has* accepted your resignation. Let me go and tell him you're going to let your resignation lie on the table till Matthieu comes home. He'll kill me if I don't make an effort to keep you.'

'No,' said Rosamond quietly, and there was that in her voice that made Thelma realise she wouldn't be able to move her. She bit her lip and Rosamond was aghast to see tears in her eyes.

'I'm sorry, Thelma, but things have happened that make it impossible for me to stay.'

Thelma checked her tears, said, 'I've had such hopes. Matthieu is such a brick. He's one of the land-loving MacQueens, but every time there's a family crisis on, he comes up trumps. This isn't his milieu at all, but he has an iron sort of discipline over himself, has such loyalty to the family and to the firm that he just pitches in.'

Rosamond said so bitterly that Thelma looked at her sharply, 'I've realised it's Family with a capital F first, foremost, always. No sacrifice too great. The sort of thing you can't fight.'

Thelma actually wrung her hands. 'There, I knew you'd quarrelled! Oh, Rosamond, don't do anything

irrevocable. You're so right for Matthieu. I could just
see you married.'

'He's not right for me, so I'm getting out from under.
And I know he's never had marriage in mind. I never
fall for the right sort of men—it must be a weakness in
me. And in any case, there's far too much money in
that family for me. Anyway, I feel life has more to offer
me. I want the chance to take up my studies again. I've
fitted into the world of fashion because I had to, but
oh, it's going to be wonderful to be free of it.'

Thelma said, bewilderedly, 'You've had big dark
shadows under your eyes all week, and something missing from your voice—that lilt. I hoped it was because you
were missing Matthieu. I still think it. Don't worry, he'll
come hiving down to Dunedin after you. That I know.'

'I won't be there after this weekend, I'll be away out
in the country. I'm asking my parents to keep my address confidential. Later, when I've sorted myself out, I
hope to get accepted for university. It will have to be
next year, I suppose. Thelma, I've so loved you and
your family. Give me a few months and I'll write to
you. I—I can't talk about it any more. Please don't tell
Barbara till you get home, but give her my love.' She
bent forward, kissed Thelma and walked out of her
office, and was glad Thelma left her alone for the rest of
the long day.

Don Yelland came to her office at eight-thirty, said
goodbye to her, wished her well. Rosamond knew he
was disappointed in her.

She was taking the Southerner early next morning.
She finished her packing, tidied the flat, then took the
key to the old lady in the next-door flat. It was a Yale
lock so she could just slam it behind her when the taxi
came. She wouldn't allow herself to feel desolate because she was leaving a place where she had known
much happiness . . . the first flowering of what had been
so lovely, so kindred, yet so false.

She went to bed dry-eyed and because she was so
exhausted with emotion, fell instantly asleep.

CHAPTER EIGHT

THE strident note of a bell roused her all too soon. Surely the night hadn't gone? She fumbled for the alarm, realised it was the telephone.

She stumbled out, switched on a light and said, 'Hullo, Rosamond Briarley here . . . who can that be?'

A voice roughened with anger said, 'Who do you think it is? Matthieu, of course.'

Still fuddled with sleep, she said, 'It can't be. Oh, don't say you're back!'

'Of course I'm not back. The conference isn't over.'

She snatched at an equal tone of anger. 'Then what on earth are you ringing at this ungodly hour for?'

'I don't care what hour it is. Anyway, we're two hours behind you here. What in hell's got into you, Rosamond? Thelma's just rung me. She tried off and on all evening, but we were in committee. I've just got in. Nice thing to be greeted with! Now what *has* got into you? Let's have it. Waiting till no head of the firm is there and flitting. Thelma said you aren't leaving any address except that of your parents. What can have gone wrong?'

'It might be a good idea to give me a chance to tell you,' said Rosamond. 'The personal angle doesn't please me, Matthieu. If it had worked out as I'd thought it would, simply a job, with no personal over-tones, I'd have stayed, of course. But you made the pace too hot. If you look back on it, coolly and calmly, you'll realise you suspicioned that. You got at me once or twice for being reserved—fair enough. I had great reservations . . . about you. I came to do a job, not get taken out by the management, fussed over, made to feel ungracious if I couldn't respond.' She paused for breath. 'Don't bellow like that! I can't make out what you say.'

His voice went right down the scale then but was so intense it was even more frightening. 'I said cool and calm be damned! That's utter rot about not being able to respond. I couldn't be wrong on that. You responded very satisfactorily. If I was there, right now, I'd make you eat those words.'

'You wouldn't, you know. There would be only a very unpleasant scene, and the situation would remain as before. Matthieu, I told you I didn't think it policy to date the management. You've taken things in far too personal a way. And in any case, you've got far too much money to appeal to me. I like things to be more equal. Now please, Matthieu, I *must* get some sleep—if I *can* get back to sleep after this. I'm off tomorrow to make a new life for myself. Don't ring me at the manse—I shan't come to the phone if you do. Very flattering, all this, of course, but you can't have your own way all the time. I'll find it very satisfying to take up some work more in my own line. I——'

'But have you thought what this will do to Grandfather? He'll be horribly disappointed that you aren't there, the granddaughter of his old sweetheart.'

Rosamond felt like screaming at him not to be such a hypocrite. That he ought to be glad she was gone, that it was going to save him a lot of trouble. What was wrong with him? Did he not like being proved wrong? Did he not fancy whoever he'd been talking to on the phone having the laugh on him because the girl he'd thought a gold-digger had simply faded out of their lives? Thrawn devil! It must be a horrible streak in Matthieu that he wanted to make the break, not her.

She steeled herself against the thought of Gaspard whom she had loved so dearly.

She said, 'Everything was on too personal a plane at MacQueen's, I found. I want to be free of it all. I just suddenly found I couldn't take it. I want my own way of life. I'm going to hang up now, Matthieu. Good-night,' and she replaced the telephone.

But Matthieu MacQueen, like Macbeth, had mur-dered sleep.

It was little wonder, therefore, that, sunk into the depths of a first-class seat on the train, she slept, to her disgust, right across the Canterbury Plains, not waking till they reached Timaru. From there, she sat up and tried to take an interest in the lovely passing scenery, the enormous paddocks, the braided rivers sweeping down valleys and across plains, dividing into dozens of streams. They crossed the tumbling Waitaki River, over the Border, they called it, from English Canterbury into Scots Otago, past the gleaming white stone build-ings of Oamaru and began to skirt the beautiful coast-line of Otago, finally running into the gentle peace of Dunedin city at something after three.

Her father viewed her luggage with surprise. 'You were brought up to travel light. Why all this?'

She chickened out on telling him so soon that she'd left Christchurch. 'Oh, a lot of this I'd rather store with you. I can't keep too much in the flat.'

As time wore on she felt less and less inclined to tell them. How surprising when as a family they'd withheld no confidences from each other. She promised herself that when they got their busy Sunday over, she would tell them. She hoped to goodness they wouldn't ask a whole crowd in to meet her.

They didn't. They came in, lit a fire because it had turned chilly, something that made Rosamond realise autumn did indeed come in April. Already the English trees in the town belt that girdled the seven hills of this gracious city were splashing great daubs of red and yellow and russet among the native trees, and the har-bour and the open sea, seen from the manse windows, held the deep blue tinge of the changing season.

Mother brewed coffee, brought in sandwiches she

must have made earlier, cut a cream sponge that was
the last word in fluffiness, served them second cups,
then leaned back in her chair and said, 'Right, Rosamond, let's have it. What's wrong?'

Rosamond managed a laugh. 'I might have known it,
Omniscient One! It's not too shattering. Drapery
doesn't satisfy me any more, that's all. I want to get
back into some sort of study. I'm giving myself a break
this year and hoping to get into university or a teachers'
college next year. I'm not going back to Christchurch,
but I didn't want to disturb you on a Sunday.'

Stephen Briarley stretched out his long legs and said,
'I've had to deal with plenty of sticky situations on a
Sunday for other people. Surely I could cope with my
daughter's, especially a daughter like you. But I can't
see there's anything wrong about it. It makes me feel a
whole heap better to know you're going back into what
you've always wanted.'

Rosamond flashed him a grateful glance, then looked
at her mother, who said frankly, 'I'm disappointed. I
thought you and this Matthieu might have——'

'Made a match of it?' Rosamond suggested, laugh-
ingly. 'Mother, there's more to life than marriage!'

'Of course, but with marriage added to a career, life
can be even sweeter.'

'Granted, but not with Matthieu MacQueen, thank
you. They're obsessed with money, that family. They go
after what they want, but you'd never be sure they
didn't feel you'd married them for money. They're still
scared someone marries the grandfather and splits their
inheritance. Matthieu was quite fond of me, but I got
fed up to the teeth. I've burned my boats. He's in Australia, Gaspard's not back yet, for another fortnight, so
I cut and ran. I'm taking a position as a governess on
an only-access-by-water sheep-station on Lake Moana-
Kotare. You'd see it, wouldn't you, when you were at
Arrowtown?'

They were silent, almost shocked, but waited for her
to finish. 'This station is across the lake and is past the

last one the road over the other side of the lake reaches.
You'll have to write me care of a private bag, Ludwigtown Post Office. It comes across by tourist launch
three times a week. They're on the telephone, though.
Not nearly as isolated as in the old days when all they
had for communication was a two-way radio.

'Mother, what are you looking like that for? Your
one ewe lamb will come to no harm. It will be a marvellous life for me. They have boats, in the plural, and a
pretty nifty launch. It's quite a community! Several shepherds, who have their own cook, a married couple
living in the old homestead, and looking after Rod
MacGilpin's brother, a single man; then in the new
house, Rod and his wife Emilie, and two little girls I'll
teach and a wee boy. I haven't met them yet, because
the girl from the neighbouring station engaged me while
she was in Christchurch—Elissa MacCorquodale of
Glen Airlie. It's only three-quarters of an hour by boat
from Strathdearn. That's the name of the one I'm going
to. It sounds familiar to me. Did we ever pass through
a place called that, on one of our tours of Scotland?
No? I was sure we must have. I know I've heard it. I
leave on Tuesday for Ludwigtown, stay overnight and
cross by the tourist bus on the Wednesday morning. It's
going to be a new and glorious life for me.'

Rosamond was still telling herself that as on Tuesday
the bus took her through the dramatic hill country of
Central Otago. Delight after delight unfolded before her
in deeply cleft gorges, snow-topped mountains, great
outcrops of rocks. She was to be met at the depot by
the headmaster of the local High School, with whom
she was to stay the night. It was like a tonic to be with
people who knew nothing of the shocks she had suf-
fered emotionally recently, and talk centred mainly on
classrooms. She loved Murdoch Gunn and his wife,
Theresa, on sight.

Come morning the tourist launch left early and
Strathdearn, straight across the lake, was one of the first

calls, though with the feast of beauty spread before her she could have stayed aboard all day. Theresa had said that Lake Wakatipu was sapphire, and Wanaka cornflower blue, but that Lake Moana-Kotare, so aptly named the Lake of the Kingfisher, was all blues and greens.

The distant shore took on shape and feature, a jetty painted scarlet jutted out into the iridescent waters, the blur of the trees became golden-brown willows that trailed their fingers in the lake, poplars like flaming torches stood proud and tall, and silver birches shivering in the breeze had leaves so golden, so sovereign-like, you almost expected them to tinkle.

Maples on the homestead lawns splashed vividly scarlet ... autumn was much more advanced down here. April ... could it be possible? At home bluebells would be carpeting the woods and daffodils would be blowing goldenly before the wind.

The pilot said to Rosamond, 'There's the new house up on the hill, all spread out to the sun, but with that huge shelter belt of macrocarpas behind it to the south where the weather comes from. You can't quite see the old homestead from here ... but you can see the drive winding up through the lindens. It dips down into a corrie. They had to build the first houses that way to give them some sort of shelter from the pitiless winds that swept down the gullies in winter, yet in summer they were scorched by the sun.

'That's where the Macks and Hugh live ... in the homestead.' He cast a sly look at her. 'I think they knew what they were doing when they got you as a governess ... they're mighty keen to get Hugh married off.'

Rosamond looked horrified. 'How ghastly! I do hope you're wrong. Matchmaking ought to be banned by law!'

He burst out laughing. 'Well, don't feel too bad right away. I believe he's overseas at present. He's a good sort, though. Oh, here they come, helter-skelter from the house ... the whole family.'

Even small Geordie was running. Rosamond was glad to see they had him on reins. She was greeted as warmly as if she'd been a long-absent sister returning. Rod was a giant of a man, Emilie tall and well-built too, but as graceful as one of the birches. Rosamond hadn't much personal luggage, but there were several boxes of books. They also unloaded the mail-bag, cases of fruit, pasteurised milk in crates, bread, some tools, a couple of tyres, some drums of oil and agricultural supplies.

There was a huge morning tea on the table, pikelets with redcurrant jelly, which Rosamond called dropscones, oatcakes still warm and crumbly, fudge cake and shortbread. To her surprise Rosamond drank three cups of tea. She still couldn't quite believe this was her and she had an idea that when she gained the sanctuary of her own room that night, the gnawing ache of missing Matthieu would start again. Meanwhile there was plenty to do here. It warmed the heart to be so needed, so welcomed.

Emilie said, 'I think you should have today off to get settled in.'

Rosamond shook her head. 'I'd like to start regular hours this afternoon. Easter will be here so soon, and though it's only a four-day break, it all cuts into time. I'll be slower with them at first, so we may have time to make up. But I'll unpack now.'

Helene bobbed up. 'Can we help with that, Miss Briarley?'

Emilie said swiftly, 'People like to unpack in private, love, not have every garment commented on.'

Rosamond laughed. 'It won't worry me. Come on, it'll be fun putting things away.' Emilie, Geordie on hip, led the way to the back of the house. 'This is quieter, away from the children. After having them all day you'll want a break, but of course when you move over

to the homestead when Hugh and the Macks get back,
it'll be better again. The girls can take you over there
after lunch, and get you familiar with the set-up.
Geordie has a sleep then so I can't leave the house.
Oh, how thankful I am you've come! Life was just too
full.'

This was a beautiful house, modern, but designed
with grace and elegance, and very labour-saving. Geordie had trucks and balls and building blocks all over the
floor, but this only enhanced the family atmosphere. A
most unfamiliar sensation of envy swept over Rosamond ... how wonderful to have your life resolved for
you, to have a handsome giant of a husband, three gorgeous children, a life of hard work, but in idyllic
scenes—oh, yes, she envied Emilie all right. And you
would never be lonely ... always someone to share the
hours with, even the night hours. Oh, stop it, Rosamond, she scolded herself. You wanted to be free.

When the children took her up through the pines and
limes of the homestead drive, she realised that here lay
a charm no modern house could hope to possess. Even
the shrubs and flowers of the garden had that indefin-
able air of having lived together harmoniously for a
very long time. All the old varieties of roses grew here,
some still gaily blooming, and the whole garden seemed
scented with the tang of rosemary, lavender, balsam,
pine. Some of the paths were neatly laid, some were just
of lake boulders, worn to stepping-stone smoothness by
the constant wash of waters for countless aeons. Others
had no stones at all, but under the carpet of brown pine
needles, the beaten hard white clay of the lake shore
gleamed through.

'It's a bitsy house,' observed Fanny cheerfully, 'but
we love it. Uncle Hugh says that like Topsy it just
growed. I think it grew and grew and grew.'

'A higgeldy-piggeldy house,' added Helene. 'We have
the funny sticky-out bit at the end. That's a very old
bit.'

'But not the oldest.' Fanny sounded superior. 'The oldest was just a but and a ben when they came out from Scotland first.'

'It's all very lovely,' said Rosamond softly. 'It not only grew, but it rooted, and if you'd moved as much as I did, because my father was a minister, you'd think that was the best thing of all.'

Part of it was stone, rough-quarried from the hillside, so that it blended in like part of the terrain, some was timbered—pit-sawn, she was to find out later—with still the curved marks of the saws on the surface, mute testimony to the gruelling hours spent sawing planks out of trees laid over deep holes in the ground.

The top floor was more elegant, with dormered windows, sparkling in the sun, and the sills were a soft blue against the white of the walls, and the frames black. Birdsong sounded about it and the music of a little brook that meandered down terraces in thin silver strands of sound.

'We've got our own entrance,' said Fanny importantly, 'so it's just like a school. We have a bell an' all. That was more for when they had children of the farmworkers here, but we still sound it every morning. If you like we'll show you over the house first. Uncle Hugh sleeps in the middle dormer over the front door, Mack and Mrs Mack in the end one, the others are guest-rooms and there are two bedrooms downstairs and another bathroom and a billiard-room. So we'll go in the front door first.'

Rosamond put out a restraining hand. 'No, I think I should wait till Mrs Mack shows me over. It's not nice to think a stranger wanders round your house when you're away, and anyway, it's so big it would take too long and I'd like to settle you at some lessons. But you can both show me where everything is and what stage you've got up to, then you can do some revision on what you did last, while I get everything ready for a full working day tomorrow.'

Fanny looked impish. 'I didn't think we'd get away

with that,' she announced cheerfully, 'but it was worth a try. Don't you even want to see the room you'll be sleeping in when they come back?'

'No.' Rosamond's voice was firm.

It was surprising how soon the children settled down. Having established that they couldn't put anything over her, they respected Rosamond and got down to it.

At night Rosamond excused herself early, said she'd have a bath and a long read. Emilie smiled. 'You're sure you aren't doing this to leave us together? Because we don't have a lot of company and we're enjoying this.'

Rosamond thought it best to be frank. 'It's partly that, but mostly because I'm tired. But I still think it's a good thing I'll have my room over there when the others get back. I think even discipline is better that way. The set-up here is good, it seems to me. The men on the station have their own quarters and aren't always sitting over you.'

Rod smiled. 'This governess knows her onions! On a place as isolated as this, where sometimes small problems can become magnified into big ones because we can't get away from each other, these things are important. It's good to have Hugh's company, but even he won't come over every night, just two or three times a week. Anyway, he'll be back in ten days' time. Pity he won't be here for Easter. Till then you're stuck with us for company, though judging by the way the lads were eyeing you, I don't think you'll be short of that. We're lucky old Grimby doesn't mind cooking for them when the Macks are away. He has his own hut and TV, otherwise their noise would get on his nerves, but he puts on some good meals for them. You must tell us when you can't stand the isolation one day longer, and we'll all have a day across in Ludwigtown. I'm told you like messing about with boats, so we'll get you used to these ones in no time at all. Main thing is we insist on absolute safety rules being observed, and never get careless about that. I'll get you out on the lake tomorrow afternoon. Emilie will have told you we start an hour earlier than ordinary schools, so that we can have a long afternoon free of lessons.'

In two days Rosamond knew she had done the right thing. In time when she got rid of this horrible and unreasonable ache for Matthieu, she should be able to enjoy this life to the full.

The children were a delight, apart from the odd hour when, like all children, they were little devils. They adopted Rosamond immediately as someone who had oodles of time to answer questions, go with them on their nature-study rambles, someone who even made them feel superior because they had to initiate her into so much farm lore and lake lore. She didn't mind them laughing at her because she was such a duffer and didn't know what they meant by crutching and tupping, flystrike and drenching, or why they called 'Wayleggo' when they sent the dogs round. 'I don't know who's teaching who,' said Rosamond, laughing, as they explained the different dogs to her, and their individual tasks.

Emilie was delighted. 'When Elissa said you'd been a compere for fashion shows for a big firm in England, I was aghast—thought she'd gone stark raving mad to have picked you. Mind you, Elissa herself was an interior decorator in Surrey, but she'd spent part of her childhood at Glen Airlie when her mother was governess to the Airlie children. But she was so certain you were a gift from the gods, in spite of never having lived in the country, I didn't like to set her back. Mind you, every holiday time you're to go down to Dunedin. We can't expect you to immure yourself here. In fact, if you wanted to do just that at Easter, you could.'

Rosamond looked horrified. 'I've only just got here! This is more like a holiday than work. That magnificent lake . . . so huge, so beautiful. I have a grandmother in Canada, who came from New Zealand originally. She once spoke of a lake she loved. I expect it was in Central, because I do know she was at Otago University.

She said it was for her the one spot beloved over all, *à la* Rudyard Kipling. She spoke of it as having blue-green waters. I'd love to think it was this one. I must ask her in a letter some time.'

Emilie's eyes sparkled. 'How lovely if it was. She'd love to think you'd come here, if it was this one. Doesn't your father know?'

'I don't think so, or he'd have said. I think it belonged to Gran's romantic past, in her student days, and she doesn't seem to have talked of it much.'

'Lots of students still come up during the vacations to work at the hotels and shops in Ludwigtown; it's very much a tourist attraction then. She could have worked there.'

'M'mm. I don't think it was a town because she said long ago to me that it was a solitary place where no roads came and there were reflections of great mountains in the lake, and, yes, the baaing of sheep upon a hundred hills.'

Emilie giggled. 'The sheep provide no clue, they're everywhere, but the rest . . . yes, it could have been any of the sheep-stations this side of the lake. Glen Airlie's had a road only a short time, but all those years ago, none of the homesteads on this side had any access, save by water. Then there's Mahanga-Puke, still, like us, with no road. That estate goes a long way back too, and even when they had only a launch once a fortnight for supplies, students loved to work there and here to earn money for another year and to get away from it all. The only other lake that's blue-green, not true blue, is Lake Tekapo up in South Canterbury. That's a sort of turquoise. Be interesting to know, wouldn't it? Do write and ask your grandmama. We've certainly got the mountains. There's very little snow on them yet, though.'

Rosamond gazed up at the symmetrical height of Mount Serenity that dominated this side of the lake. 'But it's covered on the peak.'

'It always is, but in winter the snow comes far down. But it's a dry, sparkling cold as in Switzerland, and lying facing the north as we do, we still get sun all day, most days. It's the most beautiful mountain, isn't it? I was born here. I was the one who beat the gun. The others were born in Ludwigtown. Mount Serenity has been part of my life ever since I can remember. I used to say goodnight to it every night. I thought God lived up there.'

'My aunt's name is Serena,' said Rosamond. 'Dad's sister. I asked Gran once had she called her after anyone, but she said no, it was just a name she loved. How odd if she was called after that mountain. I suppose you see it from all the other sheep-stations?'

'Yes. There's even a hint of illusion about it. From Glen Airlie and Mahanga-Puke too, it looks as if it's dead centre above each station. Same as ours . . . what's Geordie doing? I can't hear him. Oh, Rosamond, look . . . what a disaster!'

Emilie had left some green cake colouring on the bench. Geordie had shuffled a stool up to it with great stealth, and had tipped the whole bottleful into the bowl of whipped cream Emilie was going to spread on the jam and pikelets for afternoon tea. He had it on his nose, his tawny hair, his dungarees!

Rosamond swooped on him, dangled him over the sink while Emilie made swipes at him with a dishcloth which rapidly turned a most virulent colour. The two girls were helpless with laughter, Geordie purple with fury. The worst of it off, Geordie was rushed to the bathroom, held struggling while his mother ran water into the bath, then dropped him in, clothes and all.

'I have a feeling,' groaned Emilie, 'that even the bath will stay green . . . it could be indelible.' But it wasn't, it came off clothes, skin, and bath, though Geordie's hair was definitely tinged with green, and his nails were rich emerald. 'I hope it wears out of them quickly. He's a demon when I have to cut his nails.'

'It was my reminiscing did it,' said Rosamond rue-fully. 'Two of us looking after one child. You'd have fared better on your own.'

'Rubbish, we've had worse disasters than that. Look, I haven't a drop of cream left. I can't put that muck on, it looks positively evil. Times like this I yearn for a corner shop.'

'Never!' ejaculated Rosamond in horror.

The men had less aesthetic tastes, they insisted on ladling on emerald green topping and ate with gusto.

Rosamond rang the Manse that night. Her mother said, 'You sound a good deal happier than when you were here, my girl. Nothing like work for taking your mind off things. There'll always be something to do on a place like that. Isn't it a glorious lake? I envy you those views.'

'Yes, and I've a particularly good one from my room, a garden view with the lake beyond. But by now the children have shown me the room I'll have at the home-stead when the Macks get back. In fact rooms. I'm very lucky. There's what amounts to a flat attached to the schoolroom. It's the oldest part of the house, and was the original sitting-room and bedroom. I've got both. It's comfortably furnished with the old-fashioned stuff that appeals to me, and there's a toaster and electric kettle besides an open fire. I'll make my own break-fast—that'll be less bother for the Macks. I daresay the brother won't want a chattering female at the breakfast table, either. Anyway, they'd be up at the crack of dawn.

'Mother,' she added, 'I wanted to ask you is there any chance that Gran ever spent any time up here? Not necessarily this sheep-station, but did she spend any vacations up here, holidaying or working?'

She thought her mother hesitated. Perhaps she was thinking. Then she said, 'What makes you think that, Rosamond? Has someone said you remind them of Gran? Or what?'

'No, just that long ago Gran said her favourite memory was of a blue-green lake with mountains and sheep. And this is the Lake of the Kingfisher—a glorious colour. And one of the mountains is called Mount Serenity. Is it possible she called Aunt Serena after it?'

Her mother burst out laughing. 'Don't suggest that to your aunt if you're writing! She always said it was the most unsuitable name she could have been given as it was. She's such fun, but so volatile! If she thought she was called after anything as solid as a mountain, she might feel it was even less apt. You'd better ask Gran all these things yourself.'

'I will. I should have written long since. I'll write tonight . . . what did you say?' Rosamond broke off to exclaim.

'Don't shriek in my ear like that, child! I said you can ask her in person. She's coming quite soon. She's actually given up some of her committees, and she seems to be planning quite a long holiday here. Nice if she could be here in the May holidays, when you would be home. By the way, I hope you're paying this bill, not your employers . . . Sorry, love, there's someone knocking at the door. I must go—your father's out. Goodbye.'

Rosamond stood staring at the phone, regret washing over her. Oh, if only things had turned out differently! If she'd been still in Christchurch, in that lovely flat by the green-banked Avon, when Gran flew in, she could have brought her to it, and let Gaspard and Louise meet. Even if he hadn't been the one the young Louise had truly loved, who was to know what had happened? What joy it would have given Gaspard!

Emilie said, 'What's happened, Rosamond? You've gone into a trance. It sounded as if your grandmother is coming to New Zealand. Or am I wrong? You positively shrieked! But now you don't look as glad as I thought you would. I say,' she went on, 'if this does happen to be the lake she loved, she must come up here. In fact, come in any case. We're very family-minded, and I'm sure you are too. But what are you looking sad for?'

Rosamond gave herself a little shake. 'Just that I—that there's someone in Christchurch who knew Gran long ago. It would have been nice for them to meet again.'

'But that would be easy to arrange, surely? Your grandmother's very young for her age, isn't she? I mean, if she can fly alone halfway across the world, a trip to Christchurch would be nothing. I've got relations up there, with stacks of room. If she doesn't like hotels she could stay with them and——'

Rosamond shook her head. 'No, Gran goes to all sorts of conferences still, in all sorts of outlandish places, even; I can arrange it all right. Silly of me to feel like that—disappointed I wouldn't be there to meet her. It'll be great if we can get her up here. You're a darling, Emilie.'

But later, in her room, the full force of that regret hit her. If only, if only Matthieu MacQueen hadn't been such a conniving, hateful deceiver!

April went on painting the tree-girt shores of the Lake of the Kingfisher in colours that reminded Rosamond of the October she had spent with her grandparents in Canada four years ago. Yet these colours were heralding Easter. A moment of fierce longing swept over her . . . for Matthieu's presence here, for all those kindred things they had shared. But how kindred *had* he been? How much of it had been pretence to draw her away from his grandfather, who, presumably, held the money-bags and the reins in that family?

Would she never stop missing Matthieu? It was stupid. There was no future in it. She was here to build a new life for herself. One could. No one, for instance, would ever have doubted that Gran and Granddad had been happy. No, she, their granddaughter and Gran's namesake, could find happiness too. What had Gran said once? 'Happiness isn't handed to one on a golden platter, Rosamond. It's achieved.' Had Gran had a struggle to achieve it?

Rosamond was sitting on her favourite rock above the jetty, watching the small boats rocking gently on the bosom of the lake. Was it possible she had been here only ten days? She felt it had been for ever. The only cloud on the horizon was the imminent arrival of the Macks. They were coming in on the first tourist launch on Easter Saturday. They'd said, when they had rung Emilie, that that would give them time to prepare for Hugh's return the following week.

Rosamond knew it was the right thing for her to move to the homestead. Emilie and Rod must be on their own, but what if Mrs Mack didn't really like having another woman in her house? Thank goodness there was that sitting-room, but the thought of meals with someone who might resent her gave her a choking feeling already. She tried to banish that thought, and failing to do so, comforted herself with the recollection that she'd got on fine with Goldie. That comfort was succeeded by a swift nostalgia that positively pierced her . . . Goldie had even hinted that if another mistress came to that lovely home near the Millbrook Reserve she and George would retire to their own quarters. Oh, yes, she wouldn't have been unwelcome there. Oh, stop it, Rosamond, she scolded herself, don't get preconceived ideas. The Macks could be perfect darlings. She heard Emilie calling her and sprang up, running up the long steps and terrace to the house.

'I do wish Rod hadn't taken the girls to Serenity Hut. Of all things that was a ring from Elissa. Her sister-in-law and family—the ones Elissa taught when she first came to the lake—are on their way up from Dunedin for Easter and they've got Hugh with them. He arrived back in New Zealand earlier than he thought, and true to type can't wait to get here. He stayed overnight with them in Dunedin. They rang from Frankton to say they had him with them, and could someone take the launch to Glen Airlie to get him. They tried to ring us before they left home, but couldn't get us, our line was busy. Of course it wasn't, but I knew why immediately. Not five minutes ago I discovered young Geordie must have been at the phone again, and hadn't got the receiver back on. I thought it had been a nice peaceful day! I'll have to smack him next time he goes near it. I told Elissa to tell them when they arrive that Rod would come, but not early. I wonder if you'd stay in the house,' she added. 'Geordie's fast asleep. I'll saddle up and ride to the hut. And I did want to finish those new dresses for the girls. They want to wear them to Ludwigtown Church on Easter morning.'

'What's wrong with me setting off now in *Miss Serenity*?' asked Rosamond. 'I'd rather do that than carry on with the sewing, believe me! I can describe clothes, but I'm a duffer at dressmaking, and Rod mightn't want to stop what he's doing up the mountain.'

Emilie chuckled. 'They're not on the mountain, or they'd not have taken the girls. The hut's at the foot. You're right about them not wanting to stop. They're fencing, and they all want a break at Easter. It's the last holiday, bar Anzac Day, before the winter. You wouldn't be nervous, out in the boat alone?'

'No, you know I'm a fiend for the safety rules, and it's like a millpond today, and the weather report was excellent. Hugh can bring it back. I'll love it.'

Out on the lake, with the feel of the wheel under her fingers and her delight in managing it alone, Rosamond's spirits lifted as her horizons widened. Fair headlands reached out into the iridescent waters, making innumerable small bays in which, come summertime, they'd told her, were favourite picnic places. This is the life, she thought, skimming along, the sun beating down on her, the breeze of the passage lifting back the golden-brown tresses from her ears.

How much better this was than calling out the names of creations on which too many people would spend far too much money, moving among them afterwards, twittering meaningless nothings ... across there the rooftops and trees of Ludwigtown nestled into its valley, and on the dark hills above the Arrow, further away, poplars stood out like flaming torches and the larches were showing a golden leaf here and there. Right through May, she'd been told, they would be splotches of gold.

This Hugh would think her rather a scruffy governess, that word smacked of Victoriana, but up here it oughtn't to convey that . . . governesses were supposed to ride with the children, even pitch in to help putting the sheep through the mister dips in emergencies. So she hoped he'd not look askance at her well-worn jeans, saddle-stitched in scarlet, and her denim shirt worn loosely over them. It was so hot her feet were bare except for toe-jandals, though she'd put a leather jerkin on the seat for the trip home when the wind might have freshened.

Glen Airlie Bay came in sight. There was no one at the jetty or near. Of course they wouldn't expect the *Miss Serenity* so soon, as Emilie had told them Rod was up at the Hut. But the next moment three small figures, who must be Logan's nieces and nephew, came tearing down across the picnic area to the jetty. They'd shouted back as they ran, so no doubt the whole crowd would follow.

That would be Rennie in the lead, Bess, the fair one, next, and Isabel, who'd stopped to do the shouting, the dark one, last. They weren't long back from Cambridge where they'd been for the last two years. The doors of Airlie House had been flung open and quite an array of people were advancing. Rosamond had met them all on the one visit she had paid with the MacGilpin family. No doubt Hugh MacGilpin would be among them.

However, suddenly, well in front of them, a figure appeared from the direction of the men's quarters. This would be him. Rosamond, with some help from Rennie, continued tying up the *Miss Serenity*, rubbed her hands on the seat of her jeans and came up the steps to the jetty as the stranger stepped on to it.

It was an astounding moment for both as their eyes met, locked, recognised. Amazement spread over one face, horror over the other.

Then, 'Matthieu MacQueen!' gasped Rosamond, eyes wide. 'What on earth are *you* doing here?'

His nostrils tightened, his lips narrowed. 'What am *I* doing here? Coming home, of course! The question is rather what are *you* doing here. What in hell brought——'

She interrupted him, though feebly because her lips had gone dry, and the coming home phrase hadn't registered, 'I'm ... I'm the governess at the next station, Strathdearn. What do you mean——' realisation of what he'd said hit her like a broadside—'you said coming home? Oh, do you mean Glen Airlie? But how? You belong——'

He said between his teeth, 'Home? What else could that mean but Strathdearn? We MacQueens have farmed it for over a hundred years. You *must* have known. That's my launch. You must have brought it for me. What are you playing at?'

She gulped. 'I was told to meet Hugh MacGilpin. Where is *he*? Why are you here instead?'

Light seemed to dawn on him. He said, still giving the impression of gritting his teeth, 'They've always called me Hugh here. I'm only Matthieu in the business, but what in thunder——?' he took a step towards her as if he'd like to shake her. Madly embarrassed by the children as an audience, surprised into a silent ring, and miserably conscious of the party getting nearer who were going to see her shaken and shamed, Rosamond took an instinctive step backwards at the very moment a yellow streak shot between her and the edge of the jetty. She hadn't a hope of recovering her balance, her knees buckled under her, she grasped wildly at the air and disappeared backwards over the side into the deep green water.

CHAPTER NINE

THERE were yells from the children, echoed by the nearing group, and an indescribable sound from Matthieu as he dived clean in. By the time he'd come up beside her, Rosamond had recovered from the first impact of the chilly water and was shaking drops from her eyes and treading water.

As Matthieu came into position behind her and clutched her in excellent life-saving style, she made a tadpole movement away from him, so that, surprised, he let her go and she snapped furiously, 'Don't bother! I'll get myself out, thanks.'

Rennie, on his hands and knees above them, said, 'Crumbs . . . she's cross. Ben, you're in trouble and I'm scared we'll be too, for letting you off. You just go crazy.'

Rosamond looked up. 'It wasn't his fault . . . it was . . . it was just——' she glared at Matthieu, 'it was *his* fault! I got such a shock at seeing him.'

The two girls looked at each other and burst into giggles. Matthieu said, as Rosamond began to swim towards the steps with strong strokes, 'Rennie, help her up, then give me a hand. My shoes are a ton weight.'

Rosamond, alarmed, turned swiftly, but he said, 'Oh, I shan't drown. It's just damned awkward. For heaven's sake get on up.'

But she waited, and they swam side by side. He said, 'Up with you first. I'll hang on here.'

Rennie assisted Rosamond, then got his arm under Matthieu's armpit. As Rosamond gained the top she looked over into the pellucid water and said, 'My jandals came off. I'll get them,' and as Matthieu's startled face drew level with the planking on the jetty, a wet

blue streak passed him, diving cleanly and accurately to
the shingle bottom. She surfaced, transferred one jandal
to the other hand so one was free, and struck out again
for the steps, plonked them on a step out of reach of the
lapping water and clambered up unaided.

'Suffering snakes!' exclaimed Rennie, 'she *must* like
swimming. Anybody'd think it was the middle of
summer!'

'And it's certainly not,' said Matthieu, 'so we'd better
get up to the house pronto and get changed. No doubt
Elissa will give you something to change into. Here
they are, the whole clamjamfry of them. What a
moment!' He dropped his voice. 'Leave this to me. The
explanations . . . I mean that.'

Rosamond was quite glad to, for the double immer-
sion had left her teeth chattering, though that was
mostly shock at finding that Hugh MacGilpin was Matthieu MacQueen.

The others, naturally, had hurtled down when they saw
what had happened, but now they stood staring and
looking as if at any moment they'd succumb to laughter.

A tall, mannish-looking woman who Rosamond
found out later was Logan's great-aunt Claudia said
dazedly, 'It's a case of history repeating itself. That's
exactly what happened to Elissa and Logan. To Olaf
too, for that matter.'

Isabel, dark eyes twinkling, said, 'Yes, and they were
fighting too.'

This had an extraordinary effect on everyone. Elissa
said, 'But they can't be fighting! They've just—I mean,
they don't know each other.'

'Oh, don't they?' asked Rennie with great relish.
'That's what *you* think. They sure do. Uncle Hugh said,
"What the hell are *you* doing here?" and then——'

'That'll be enough, Rennie,' said Matthieu. 'We
weren't fighting, it was sheer surprise. And Rosamond
got such a shock, she stepped backwards and that
stupid animal Ben shot round behind her just as she
was recovering her balance.'

'It looked like fighting to me,' said Bess, quietly, but not quite quietly enough.

'What did you say, Bess?' asked her courtesy uncle.

Bess said in the pure English accent she'd picked up in her two years in Cambridge, 'I really don't think I should repeat it.'

'Thank heaven for that,' said her mother devoutly. 'Consider it unsaid, Hugh. But for goodness' sake satisfy our curiosity and tell us where you met. Then we'll rush you up to the house.'

His voice was bland, confident. 'Oh, Miss Briarley took a temporary job in our shop when she arrived from England. She wouldn't have the faintest idea I was really a farmer, of course. This is just one of those coincidences you don't believe in books, but are always happening in real life. She didn't like the shop life and wanted to get away from it. Can't say I blame her. I'm the same way myself, as you know. So now ... I guess some of your clothes will fit her, Elissa. It may have been a sunny day, but it is autumn and that lake water's icy.'

They all trooped up to the house. The children were keen not to miss a word. They knew darned well there was more behind this. Rosamond thought she'd scream at all the oohing and aahing over the coincidence. She kept reasonably close to Matthieu to make sure their stories tallied.

Elissa said, 'I'm trying to remember what I said when I engaged you. About the set-up, I mean. Trust me! I'm getting to be an addlepate.'

Rosamond said, 'No, it was just that I got a wrong impression. You said there was a schoolroom in the old homestead where the bachelor brother lived, that Mr and Mrs Mack looked after him and that I'd have a room there. Let's all say what a small world it is. I took it for granted that it was Rod's brother, a partner on the farm. It's been frantically busy since I've been there, and all that was ever said about this Hugh was that he was overseas. I assumed it had been a world trip, but even if they'd said Australia I wouldn't have connected

him with MacQueen's Mr Matthieu. I suppose if I'd
explored the old homestead I might have seen a photo
or something, but I told the girls I didn't think it fair to
look through a house in the absence of those who lived
there. I suppose sooner or later it would have come out,
but I've been there so short a time.'

Matthieu had other clothes in his case and disappeared into the men's quarters to have a warm
shower. Elissa ran one for Rosamond, and rubbed her
hair dry. 'Mother will make us a pot of tea. What a
blessing your hair dries like this and doesn't need setting. Here's some make-up. Do you know,' she added, 'I
like that outfit better on you than on me. It's a change
to have green trews when we wear so many blue jeans,
isn't it? I'm going to put this big natural wool jersey on
you. Nobody swims in the lake in April. And take these
scuffs. Your feet look smaller than mine, but size isn't
so important with these. Oh, you look glowing now.'

'I feel glowing . . . and a prize idiot,' said Rosamond.
'I needn't have reacted quite like that.'

'Oh, not to worry, it was mostly Ben's fault. It mostly
is, but we do love him. He used to belong to Rennie and
the girls, but we had him while they were in England
and it's a shame to send him back to town now. They've
ordered a spaniel for the children. Mind you, Ben's a
menace to life and limb, but he's very clever the way
he's picked up some stock skill from the other dogs. No
real training, but he copies them. Now, come on.'

Rosamond's head was whirling. One moment she was
scared she'd contradict the impression Matthieu was
giving of their former acquaintance, the next she was
wishing it could go on indefinitely, because he wasn't
going to spare her with his tongue when he got her on
board the *Miss Serena* again.

The moment for departure came, they cast off, waved
farewells, headed out into the lake. Matthieu was at the
wheel, of course, his sodden clothes and ruined leather
shoes on one of the seats, mute reminders of the
mishap.

He turned and said, 'Come over here and tell me *exactly* how you came to apply for that job, now we haven't an audience.'

Rosamond came obediently, but her answer was anything but meek. 'It's all your fault, every bit. You left that torn-out advertisement sitting on your desk. Shona told me you'd left some clippings there for me to file. I scooped that up too, saw some of our scatter-ads in a column, trimmed it up, and gave it to the girl to file. The ad for the governess caught my eye. I expect you put it in for your sister. It sounded like heaven to me. I could get away from it all, which was exactly what I needed to do right then. It wasn't a whopping coincidence as the others think, just a natural chain of events. Unfortunately.'

She looked at him sharply. 'You have the air of not believing me.'

'Oh, I believe you saw the ad and that was why you applied, but I know your real reason for coming up here. Why can't you be honest?'

Anger sharpened her voice. 'I think you'd better tell me what you mean!'

'Pretending still, aren't you? That you had no other motive. You came up here to be near Jeff Vane and his precious motels. I think you want to test your feeling for him. You just made that excuse to Don and Thelma that I was embarrassing you with my attentions ... to put it in an old-fashioned way.'

'Jeff? I haven't seen him or heard from him since that day in my office when he rang and I told him I wasn't interested. He's probably back in Auckland by now.'

His voice was dry it rasped. 'Oh, come, surely you can do better than that! He was in the store in Frankton when I stopped to phone. He didn't see me—I took care of that. Not that I had any idea then you were in the district. I just didn't want him asking after you, seeing I hadn't the faintest idea where you were, in the South.'

Rosamond said intensely, 'I'm used to being believed. Most people are inclined to believe the children of the manse. I didn't come here because of Jeff.'

'Then why did you tell Verna that that was why you were going South?'

She was aghast. She was betrayed out of her own mouth. Matthieu looked at her and laughed. Not a triumphant laugh, though, it sounded bitter, rueful.

She said numbly, 'All right, you win. I lied. But not to you just now. Only to Verna, because I didn't want her to guess I was running away from you. It was as much for you as for me because it's horrible for heads of firms to be talked about. Any store is a hotbed of gossip.' He didn't answer and she burst out, 'Even had I not told that lie you wouldn't have believed me now. You aren't a believing sort of person. Look what you thought about your grandfather ... that perhaps he'd strayed, long ago. I'm more than sure he didn't. I think he'd just gone off to lick his wounds ... like an animal, he had to be alone.'

His voice was very level. 'Touché. But I don't think that now. The day Grandfather got back he told me about that. About finding out mischief had been made between him and *your* grandmother.'

Rosamond gulped. 'Did he tell you who made it?'

He did. '*My* grandmother. His wife.'

'And?'

'When she was out of danger he thought he'd go off to Akaroa while she was in hospital still to think things out. He was going to ring from there to say he'd not be in for a day or two. He got out of the bus, went down to the waterfront, thought he'd book in at a hotel shortly, and he completely lost his memory. He sat on, under the trees, and fell asleep. He got robbed. Fortunately they missed some notes he had in a waistcoat pocket, so he went to a hotel, made up a name, spent a few days there.

'He knew he'd have to go to a doctor sooner or later, but kept postponing it. He walked into a drapery shop to buy a change of clothing—his case had been pinched too—and the man cried, "Why, hullo, Gaspard, I haven't seen you for years," and it all came flooding back. He was darned glad to have avoided publicity.'

Rosamond didn't answer; she couldn't. Matthieu said, 'Well, say something.'

'How can I? She was your grandmother. I'd hate to hear anything like that about mine. I can't comment.'

He said roughly, 'Did you suddenly find out who it was who made the mischief? Did it make you feel you couldn't trust *me*? Answer me, did you?'

She thought of what she'd heard him say on the phone to someone, of what he'd told Verna and her mother. It was odd, he was just as angry that *she'd* dumped *him* as if he hadn't planned the reverse. Just an instance of the high and mighty male perhaps. Pride. Why should she trust him?

She said slowly, 'I didn't analyse it as much as that. In any case, I've known since that weekend on the Isle of Wight that it was your grandmother. But yes, I don't trust you, Matthieu. I neither trust you nor like you. You wanted an answer. That's it.'

She saw his hands whiten on the wheel. Had she looked at his face she'd have seen that whiten too.

After quite some time, he said, 'Funny . . . I've never thought it at all reasonable, even though I'm of Scots descent myself, for the unforgiving attitudes that descended through the clans. Not with all people but some. Like some Macdonalds saying: "Never trust a Campbell." It's all wrong. But I've got Ellie MacQueen's blood in my veins. I even look like her. So all this happens.'

Rosamond said, seemingly irrelevantly, 'So Gaspard *was* my grandmother's true love after all. This would be the lake they met by, fell in love with each other here. I hadn't known he'd farmed here too, but I suppose he must have. I assumed it had been someone else. It seemed so far from the world of drapery. No one had ever mentioned Strathdearn.'

He said, 'Except that night at Christchurch, when Goldie served the saddle of mutton.'

'Oh, that was it! I asked my parents if we'd ever passed through a place called Strathdearn when we holidayed in Scotland. I wish it had rung a clearer bell. But even then I mightn't have guessed. Matthieu, if you'd been more open and told me you were a farmer, just helping out in the shop because Pierre was away as well as Gaspard, none of this would have happened. I wouldn't have come here. Why didn't you?'

'Because this is the backblocks. We haven't even got a road. And you'd lived in London and Southampton. I said I'd got something to tell you. How could I guess you had a yen for the great open spaces? Or is this just a flash in the pan? Will the novelty pall and you'll flit once again?'

She couldn't help it. He was still pretending. He didn't want to confess he'd been making a fool of her. She said, with a touch of real malice in her voice, 'You were afraid I'd be more attracted to a draper, to the world I knew. Perhaps you even thought if I didn't fancy a horny-handed son of the soil, I might have had a shot at your grandfather. You said I was a marriage-or-nothing girl.'

'Oh, don't talk such rubbish!'

She allowed a hint of laughter to creep into her tone. 'I've come too close to the bone, have I? Well, Matthieu MacQueen, the lake miles are lessening. We'd better work out what we're going to do. Would you like me to tell Emilie I can't, after all, take the solitude of the lake? I've no wish to stay here to embarrass you if you feel you can't take my presence in your house after all this.'

His lip curled. 'You've a habit of cutting and running whenever things get too much for you, haven't you?'

Her hands clenched. 'That is entirely uncalled for! Leaving Christchurch because of you was the first time I've ever run out on anything. But I didn't care for the personal element that crept into the situation at Mac-Queen's. I felt it was better for everyone if I took off, then it could never come to a clash between your grandfather and yourself over me.'

There, he could pick up that challenge if he liked. She would have gained satisfaction had he looked guilty. But he was silent. Why?

Finally, in the most flabbergasted tones, he said, 'Why on earth should I fall out with him over you? He'd have relished the way things were heading, the way I *thought* they were heading.'

Rosamond said, exasperated, 'I'll leave you to work that one out.'

More silence. His knuckles were taut on the tiller. The very bones were showing under the skin. The silence got her.

She said, 'I don't like being manipulated. I've been put in a very false position. All sorts of things have been imputed to me. You know what you thought in Southampton. I've had eyebrows raised over that sumptuous flat. People have thought me a gold-digger, and I couldn't stand it. I had to get away. I wanted to come to people who didn't care about money, who would value one's services and just pay an adequate wage and I wouldn't need to wonder all the time if my motives were in question . . . and of all the horrible luck, I spotted that advert! It's hideous!'

She paused to control a tremor in her voice. 'I wouldn't even tell dear Thelma where I was going, just said my mother would know where I was, and would forward any mail. The only one I told. . . .' She stopped as light dawned. She whirled round from his side and came to face him, standing with her back to the bows, 'Matthieu! You must have known I was here . . . you *must*! In the letter I left with Mr Yelland for your grandfather, I told him I was taking a job at a place in the high country called Strathdearn, on Moana-Kotare. I asked him to keep it in strictest confidence, that I didn't want you to know. I said things had become too personal between us. But when he read it, he knew I was coming here, *to your home*. He *must* have told you.

No one could have resisted that. Ohhhh!' She put her hands to her head and groaned.

Matthieu's eyes met hers, steadily, convincingly. 'No need for all the histrionics. You don't know my grandfather. I could choke him for not preparing me. Now I know why the old beggar was chuckling away in his office after he'd read your letter. He'd think: "Let Matthieu go down there all unsuspecting . . . what a meeting . . . and be damned to the pair of them." He'll have the nerve to ring me up and expect me to chuckle too.'

She said passionately, 'You are not to tell him off about it! I won't have it. It's the very thing I wanted to avoid. You're just to take it as a joke against us.'

'Who are you to dictate to me?' he demanded.

'I'm not thinking about you. Gaspard is an old man. He had enough trouble in his own life without having ructions with his grandson now.'

All of a sudden their mutual anger seemed to die down. They were cutting through scenes of superlative beauty . . . a sunset splashing the lake with reflected glory, and lighting up every silvery peak with colours that seemed to belong to another world.

When Matthieu spoke again his tone was flat, tired. 'Not long to go. We have to work out how much we'll tell them. They're going to pick immediately that you aren't dressed as you were when you left. Ben can be the villain of the piece, not me. You came to Christchurch, intending to go to Dunedin to your people, but took on a job with us temporarily, and you'd been there so short a time it wasn't worth mentioning. You thought I was Rod's brother. We needn't let them know we ever went out together. I'll play it cool with Grandfather—might even make myself chuckle over it with him. At least if we take it this way, we don't have to embark on embarrassing explanations as soon as I get home. Heaven knows what'll come out in days to come, but we'll be better able to cope with it then. But watch your tongue, Rosamond. I want no disharmony at Strathdearn.'

'Suits me,' she shrugged. 'I left Christchurch rather than create disharmony in a family firm. I'd just love to take off, but Emilie is so delighted to have a governess and I just love Fanny and Helene. Oh, what a fool I've been, a blind fool! I'd have been bound to find out had I been here longer than a week or two . . . Emilie is spelt the French way, Fanny isn't Frances as I'd thought, but Fanchon, Helene is pronounced the French way, Ay-len . . . your grandfather said it was a tradition because of his mother that French names have descended. If you'd had a road coming here, of course, the mailbox would have been marked MacQueen and I'd have known on arrival, but all the mail comes in a private bag marked Strathdearn. I take it you only help out in the shop in emergencies?'

'That's it. Grandfather had so many frustrations in his own life, he wouldn't influence either my father or his grandsons in that matter. I know a bit more about it now, since he told me of the way Grandma had turned his life topsy-turvy. It wasn't just the mischief she made; she set to work, once she'd got rid of Louise, to marry him, catching him on the rebound, then proceeded to winkle him out of Strathdearn and the life he really loved. She persuaded him the children would have a better life in Christchurch where he could partly inherit, partly buy out his very old uncle to whom it belonged.

'He flung himself into money-making and it nearly turned him into a despot. Then came Ellie's confession and it stopped him in his tracks. He told me that oddly enough they were happier after that. It must have softened her as well as him. He didn't allow her to rule my father's life. She wanted him to follow in Gaspard's footsteps. But instead, Dad was allowed to carve out his own life, which was in the political field.

'She was good to us during our school holidays, according to her lights. For our spiritual needs, if I can call them that, we turned instinctively to Grandfather. He was good at explaining things to boys. We always worked at the store for some part of our vacations. It

was the breath of life to Pierre, but not to me or Emilie.
We came down here a lot. Rod's father was manager.
So when they need me, I take my turn at the shop.'

His voice had retained the flat tone during the whole
recital. It was just to clear the decks and to prepare her
for the play-acting that lay ahead. A wave of unbearable regret washed over Rosamond. Why couldn't it
have been different? If there'd not been so much money
involved to make Matthieu MacQueen suspect everyone's motives, it would have been easier. She stemmed
back the thoughts. She must be as matter-of-fact as he
was.

'Well, that's it,' she said. 'Very neatly put. At last I'm
in the picture as far as this set-up is concerned. None of
this last hideous complication would have occurred had
you been frank with me over your real occupation. I
recall now you checked Thelma when she was about to
tell me something—this situation, I guess. It needn't
have mattered.'

'I've told you my reasons. You must know what I
had in mind. I thought a girl who'd always lived in
cities wouldn't consider marrying a high-country farmer
lacking even a road to his door.'

Rosamond had to clamp her lips together to stop the
angry words. What he really meant was that he wanted
nothing to prevent her looking favourably on him, so
that when his grandfather returned, she would have no
idea of trying to win the old man's affections. Later, she
supposed, he would have jilted her.

They began to come into Strathdearn Inlet. She knew
a tremor of fear at what lay ahead.

They were all at the jetty to meet the one who'd been
away from the station so long. Emilie noticed Rosamond's change of clothing before they even tied up.
She cried out across the narrowing stretch of water,
'Rosamond . . . you've been in the lake! Oh, dear, was it
coming or going? What happened? I *knew* I shouldn't
have let you go alone.'

Matthieu said, 'Sis, don't worry. She was on the jetty at Glen Airlie when that mad Benjamin took the legs from under her. I decided to play the hero and dived in most gallantly, but it was all wasted. She swims like a fish, didn't seem to mind the cold, and *I* was the one who had to be assisted ... my shoes got waterlogged. One of life's more humiliating moments. Anyway, how are you, Clan?'

Emilie was laughing. 'Well, for sure you'll never forget the first time you met!'

Quite irresistibly Matthieu's and Rosamond's eyes met and to the surprise of both of them, they laughed. Matthieu said hurriedly, 'Well now, that's another story ... incredible as it may seem, she was working for me for a few weeks at the shop and of course had no idea I was a son of the soil, and none of you, dumb animals that you are, as much as mentioned my surname. The poor girl thought she was meeting one Hugh MacGilpin. If Ben *hadn't* scuttled her she'd probably have fallen in just the same, from sheer surprise. Right, Rod, give us a hand.'

The girls received him boisteroulsy, as befitting a fond uncle. Geordie, however, had completely forgotten him, because a few months is a long time when you're not quite two. The coincidence of Rosamond having worked at the shop occupied the conversation all the way up to the house, perched on its lake terraces.

Matthieu must have worked it out by now that some time his grandfather might be ringing Emilie, and that therefore she would wonder at his secrecy, for he said, 'It wasn't all coincidence. Grandfather called on Harry Dellabridge when he was in Southampton, and in the course of a fashion parade there he was introduced to Miss Briarley because she was planning on joining her parents in Dunedin. Naturally Grandfather said if she wanted a job she could have one in Christchurch, with us. But she felt she wanted to see some real New Zealand life, not just exchange one city job for another. Not that I knew any of this, of course, till I got back from Australia and found she'd left. Miss Briarley, now we're going to be living in the same house, I'd better call you Rosamond, do call me Matthieu.'

It was cleverly done, but Rosamond could have hit him. He was finding it far too easy. She wasn't. But then it came easy to him to act a part. She switched her mind away from their more tender scenes. They had been real to her and just a plan to him. At that moment it hit her that it couldn't have been his sister he'd been speaking to on the phone that day. If it had been, Emilie would have known very well who she was. Who, then?

There was such a lovely family atmosphere at dinner-time and afterwards that she had a great sense of un-reality. She couldn't fault Matthieu's attitude to the children, crawling round the floor with Geordie on his back, anxious to have him accept his uncle again, not minding the constant interruptions of Fanny and Helene as they brought him all their recently acquired treasures or accomplishments, asked innumerable questions.

His considerable luggage proved exciting for every-one, toys from the Toy Department for the children, though not too many or so luxurious that he could be accused of spoiling them; lines of under and outer wear for Emilie and Rod; a whole boxful of heavy-knit farm jerseys for the men which they'd get tomorrow, several parcels for Mr and Mrs Mack.

He picked up a small parcel, saying, with a dryness only Rosamond would notice, 'I thought you'd have a governess by now if Elissa had been lucky with the applicants, so I thought I'd better have something for her too. I knew she could be anything from twenty to sixty, so I played safe. It's not exciting, Miss Briarley—I mean Rosamond—for anyone as glamorous as you, but you'll have to put up with it.'

She managed to say, as any strange governess would have, 'But how kind of you, Mr Matthieu—I mean

Matthieu. What a very nice thought,' and peeled off the paper to reveal quite a choice writing-case in pigskin.

He laughed. 'Well, I remembered that in this isolated spot we do anything at all to keep our governesses happy and satisfied with their lot. No sacrifice is too great.'

Fanchon looked up with the blue eyes Rosamond now realised were just like Gaspard's and said innocently, 'You won't have to do anything to keep this one here, Uncle Hugh, she just loves us and loves Strathdearn. She can't imagine anyone ever wanting to leave the lake. And she helps with the dishes and the cooking. Mum says she's a gem.'

He patted his niece on the head. 'Then it's over to us to make quite sure it stays that way, isn't it, poppet? Emilie, if you aren't airing the homestead till tomorrow, I'd better just sleep here tonight.'

Rosamond found it hard to fall asleep. It was impossible to believe that one wall separated her from Matthieu MacQueen, no doubt sleeping flat out next door. She couldn't guess at what lay ahead. Or how she would be able to live at such close quarters with him. But at least now he must know she had no designs on the MacQueen money.

Breakfast ought to have been an ordeal but wasn't somehow. Autumn sunshine spilled in through the long kitchen-living-room with its floor-to-ceiling windows, and ranch-slider doors that gave out on to the terrace, fenced off so that small Geordie couldn't stray down to that beautiful but dangerous lake. The sun winked on the brass edges of the huge Visor fireplace where at nights huge logs of driftwood from the lake shore burned and twinkled their reflections on the amber bowls of the wall-lights.

Emilie had struck a rich note of blue on the Welsh dresser where a dinner-set Rosamond had at first taken for willow-ware was set out. But it was a valuable

Doulton set, with a Norfolk Broads design patterned all
over it. Certainly you had to step high, wide and handsome over the blocks, cars, trucks and cotton-reels
Geordie was playing with, and before subsiding on to
one of the Lazy-boy rockers you were wise to dislodge
one or other of the cats, but it was a glorious room, a
family room, the heart of the house, designed to bring
the whole lake scene into the indoors. The curtains, in a
rich gold, were drawn back all day long and one's eyes
constantly lifted to the paradise outside, the willows,
rusty-brown now, clustered symmetrically about the
edge, the poplars grew brighter every day, looking as if
some artist had painted them thickly with oils as golden
as the molten sun itself, or, as Ron Gordon over at
Thurlby Domain had once put it, poetically, as if all the
gold of the region, deep down and unobtainable, had
transformed itself into living metal.

Geordie had eaten an immense breakfast of rolled
oats porridge, toast and Marmite and milk, but he was
never averse to cadging extras. He trotted round to
Rosamond's chair, looked beguiling, lifted an angelic
countenance and said hopefully, holding out his arms,
'Toast? For Geordie?'

She looked at Emilie for permission, lifted him up,
spread honey on a square inch, popped it into his
mouth, looked down on him and suddenly, to her em-
barrassment, her eyes filled.

Startled, Emilie exclaimed, 'Rosamond! What's the
matter?'

Rosamond blinked rapidly, colour rising, and said,
'I'm being stupid. I've over-active tear-ducts, that's all.
It's . . . it's just that at this age they're so beautiful, so
trusting . . . so little makes them happy, and you hope
life will deal gently with them . . . oh, I'm being absurdly
sentimental! Change the subject, someone, please.'

Fanny obliged. 'Mum, can we all help clean out the
homestead . . . seeing it's a holiday? We've done the
schoolroom, but it'd be fun to do out Rosamond's

sitting-room and her bedroom ... and Uncle Hugh's, of course.'

Talk became general, to Rosamond's relief. She'd made what excuse she could, but it had been more than that. It had swept over her how like Matthieu little Geordie was ... the sturdiness, the well-set ears, his all-over brownness, the tawny-brown eyes, the darker brows, the hair, just a stubble, as Goldie had said on that long ago happy, happy evening when she and Matthieu had sat beside the waters of the miniature chine, and in her imagination she had seen a little boy, not much older than Geordie, with his great-grandmother, Margot Somers from the Isle of Wight, being amused while his baby sister's funeral was in progress.

Rod and Matthieu went off to see the men, looking alike in their plaid shirts, shabby farm cords, heavy boots ... they didn't get on too well with the home-stead cleaning till after an early lunch Geordie went to sleep and Rod offered to be in the house, at his desk, attending to farm accounts and records.

The men were having most of Easter off, and had gone off to Ludwigtown on the tourist launch. Rosamond was surprised when Matthieu came in to help them with the preparations for the Macks' return, wielding a mop-o-matic with a deft touch that spoke of practice. 'Not that Mrs Mack would approve. I only get away with this when she's on holiday. She's a down-on-your-knees-with-a-scrubbing-brush type, but this is quicker. It's only surface dirt anyway, after being unused for a month. It's the longest holiday the Macks have ever taken, and they deserve every moment of it. Emilie, I'll carry that upstairs for you.'

Emilie saw Rosamond and said, 'Come on up and see what I've got done up here already,' so Rosamond had to go. She was really happier in her own quarters, with the girls. The less she was with Matthieu, the less nerve strain for both of them.

She followed them into what was obviously Matthieu's room. All his school photos were ranged round the wall, his prizes occupied a shelf of the well-filled bookcases, a cricket bat and racquet stood in one corner, half a wall was devoted to prints of native birds, and the window looked out towards Mount Serenity.

Emilie said, 'Now, if only you'd let the children show you round, you'd have known he was your former boss. When the school photos leave off, the farm photos begin ... Look, Hugh in the shearing-shed, Hugh breaking in one of the wild horses, Hugh on the tractor, on the header, out on the hill, mustering.'

'Yes, I wish I'd known,' said Rosamond.

Fanchon called them. 'Mum, Dad wants you on the phone. He can't find some lists.'

When she'd gone Matthieu said, 'Why do you wish you'd known?'

She faltered in her reply, finally said, 'I don't know. I had to make some answer.'

'You do know. Because you'd have fled before I got here.'

Her voice was as flat as his had been yesterday. 'I might have wanted to, I don't know that I would have. Emilie works so hard and enjoys it all so. Her days are far too busy. To add lessons too would be unthinkable. Anything extra I do is appreciated. She almost waxed lyrical the day she found she'd underestimated her bread order and I made some simple Irish soda bread. So I might just have thought you could put up with my presence.'

'Interesting ... now I'd thought it was *you* couldn't stand *my* presence.'

As if she'd not heard him she said, 'My grandmother taught me to make that—the Irish soda bread. I wonder if she learned how up here, in the day before deep-freezers. I think now she must have been here, in this very house.'

'She was.'

Rosamond looked at him sharply. 'How do you know? For sure?'

'Grandfather told me about it. We had a day or two before Pierre got home. She came up here on a university vacation, to take over lessons, for the rest of the school year, for the shepherds' children. His mother loved Louise and barely tolerated Ellie, my own grandmother. She recognised Ellie for what she was, he said, ambitious, one who'd want to take her son away from the lake. No one was more upset than Margot when Gaspard and Louise parted and Louise went to England. So she taught here too, and now you.'

'How strange to think that I sit—probably—in the very chair she sat in, and taught from the same table.'

He said, 'If you hadn't fouled things up and if she came out here for a visit, she might have had a very happy time up here, reliving the past. Perhaps even—oh, never mind that.'

So he felt Gran couldn't be invited here now. So she kept quiet about Gran's coming visit to Dunedin. She had to tamp down her resentment. She felt like hurling her knowledge of what he'd plotted in his face. Tell him it was his fault, the fouling up. But he still went on pretending! But she held her tongue. Much more dignified, much less revealing, to have him think it was merely that she wasn't interested romantically in any MacQueen or in MacQueen money.

She said, 'I must get back to the girls, goodness knows what they're up to. Their zeal exceeds their gumption sometimes. I just love that little suite downstairs, more so now I know Gran had it as her domain. And——' she stopped.

He lifted a tawny eyebrow. 'And——?'

'And under the circumstances, that private sitting-room is a godsend.'

'Because you won't have to endure my company?'

'Because it won't impose mine on you and the Macks.'

Easter passed in the same dreamlike, unreal state. Autumn, not spring, an immense lake to look out upon instead of the Solent; not walking to church along flagged pavements, but crossing kingfisher-blue waters in a launch early in the morning, and attending church in Ludwigtown, and spending the whole day with the Gunns at the Rectory.

By the end of the following week, Rosamond was aware that there was a new threat on the horizon ... Emilie had developed a matchmaking glint in her eye, and she even suspected Rod of the same thing. It all added up ... happily married people had this trait ... here was a girl who loved the lake, didn't mind the loneliness, had been brought up to turn her hand to most things ... the children loved her, which was half the battle, and if they could possibly marry her off to the bachelor brother, they'd have someone to supervise the correspondence lessons for keeps!

Mrs Mack was as bad. Rosamond's fears there had been groundless. She was the happy-go-lucky sort, a comfortable, sonsy woman. She was doing a fine job here, though for just as long as she was needed, she informed Rosamond meaningfully one day. 'My son-in-law has a farm at Akaroa and has put aside a corner of it for us to build on when we retire. It will be ideal for my husband ... he'd pine away if he had to retire in town.' Rosamond made a vague reply, as if it really meant nothing to her.

She was extremely cagey about any invitations the Macks gave her to sit with them in the evenings. She had her little sitting-room with its cosy old-fashioned register grate, which she could pile up with pine-cones, resinous and aromatic. When Mrs Mack protested that she spent too many evenings alone, she laughed, said, 'I'm a loner, very fond of my own company. The reading I get through is terrific. I've a fair bit of prep to do for the girls, keeping one step ahead of them after being away from such things for so long, and I'm revelling in it.'

She looked up to see Matthieu standing in the doorway with an unreadable look on his face. As he caught her look he said, 'Rod asked me to give you your riding lesson today. He's away up at the Serenity Hut with a couple of the men. I've time and I'm quite happy to do it. He tells me you're coming on well. Will two-thirty do? Straight after school?'

She said swiftly, 'It's very good of you, Matthieu, but I'm skipping it today. I just don't feel up to it. I'm still a bit nervous of something moving underneath me, something unpredictable. I'm much happier at the wheel of a car or a launch. I've decided to give my nerves a chance to steady again.'

Mrs Mack promptly disappeared. Matthieu came across to her. 'You're chicken, aren't you? Chickening out because you're nervous of me, not the horse.'

'What if I am? Surely I can please myself in the matter of riding instructors. I find it's something one needs to concentrate on, to feel at ease, calm. A horse knows immediately if one is unsure.'

He laughed, and for the first time since he had come here the old audacious light was back in his eyes. 'And of course you don't feel calm when I'm about! I disturb you . . . good!'

'Oh, leave me alone!' she snapped, and walked off to her room. What a sanctuary this was! She had her breakfasts here, her lonely evenings. Sometimes she caught herself listening for the sound of Matthieu's footsteps, but they never paused outside her door. At least he respected her privacy. In time, surely, she would learn to be indifferent to him.

CHAPTER TEN

LATER that day Emilie prevailed upon her to spend the evening with them. Rosamond accepted because when the men returned at dusk, which settled down early these May nights, she'd heard them ask Matthieu if he would join them in a game of cards. So when Emilie rang, she accepted without as much persuasion as usual.

Emilie said, 'Rod has informed me he's hardly seen me out of trews since the nights got colder, so I felt quite ashamed. It's so easy to slip into that habit. I wouldn't if Mother was here. She liked me to change into a dress for dinner, though since I had Geordie, it's inviting disaster to do so till he's bathed and in bed. So to please His High-and-Mightiness, I'm going to wear that new blue dress Matthieu brought down with him. Thelma has my measurements, you know, and frequently sends down things she feels I'd like.'

Rosamond said, 'If Rod feels like that he mightn't want me around!'

'Don't be silly. In a place like this we need company, and even Hugh won't be over tonight. He's been roped in for a card game with the men.'

Rosamond thought she would wear her rose-coloured velvet. She had worn it only once before. Yes, it was quite good to be dressing up. Not a really long skirt, it was quite suitable for a friendly informal evening in a farmhouse, yet rather a morale-lifter in the way it suited her, and it was good to be out of tartan or cord trews and bulky knitted sweaters.

The path between the houses wasn't too rough for these shoes, either. You got tired of brogues. The dress was simply cut, with a scooped-out oval neckline edged with a trimming that looked like soft white fur, and it bordered the three-quarter sleeves too. She picked up the jet necklace and bracelet, tried them against it—oh, just perfect!

She brushed her golden-brown hair till it belled round her shoulders in shining tresses, touched a little colour to her cheeks because they seemed pale tonight, added lipstick in a soft rose that matched the velvet, dabbed behind her ears with a white rose perfume Matthieu had given her once. Oh, bother, don't start thinking about him again, she scolded herself.

She picked up a white fleecy coat, slipped her arms into it, walked through the schoolroom and out of that entrance. The night was coated with stars and a pale moon was already riding high above the lake waters and there was that wine-like clarity about the atmosphere that made her realise that in the Southern Hemisphere May, you were slipping into winter, not summer.

The pine needles were cushiony under feet as she walked, the tang of them, and the tang of the blue-gums adding to her sense of a new world. It could have been an enchanted world if only—she shut her mind to that ever-intruding thought, that traitor desire.

She stopped on the lowest terrace and looked across to the golden lights of Ludwigtown ... then a male figure was silhouetted against the lake, coming up from the jetty. She called out, 'Having a last-minute stroll, Rod?'

Matthieu's voice answered her, 'Yes, but not Rod. Well met by moonlight, stranger.'

In a moment he was beside her. She said intensely, 'It's because we *aren't* strangers, because we know too much about each other that it isn't a well-met-by-moonlight encounter. What are you doing here? I thought you were in the men's quarters.'

'Well, I'm not, fair Rosamond, and I can please myself where I go and where I come. Don't be so absurd. We ought to have buried the hatchet long ago. We're going in to the harmonious atmosphere of my sister's house. We're going to keep it that way. We're not going to utter double-edged remarks hoping that we can get a dig in at each other unnoticed or understood by the others. It doesn't work. Even children can pick up undertones. I shouldn't say *even* ... I think they're the least likely to be deceived. Fanchon said to me today, "I wish Rosamond liked you better ... did you growl at her when she worked in the shop for you?" That settled it for me. It's over, Rosamond, this hostility. Whatever bee you got in your bonnet has just buzzed out. We're starting again, wiping the slate clean, burying that hatchet. Oh, heavens,' he sighed, 'I'm uttering platitudes by the yard! Here's the door. By the time we close it behind us, the era of hostility is no more. We're all going to play Scrabble.'

Rosamond was bereft of speech. It gave her the most curious feeling. As if in losing the power to utter, she'd lost the power to believe he'd ever hatched that malicious plot on his grandfather's behalf.

Matthieu took her into the big living-room with his hand under her elbow. 'Here we are,' he said, as if the invitation had originally included them both. She couldn't create a scene in front of these two dear people and well he knew it. The audacious gleam was back in his eye again. 'And doesn't she look beautiful? And don't you, my charming sister? Both doing credit to the drapery house of MacQueen's Limited!'

Emilie waved a hand round the room. 'And doesn't this look beautiful too ... not so much as a crayon, a block, or a piece of Lego in sight!'

At that moment her brother put a foot on some wretched tiny toy tank, so well camouflaged it blended completely into the gold and green carpet, and he shot forward at an alarming rate on one leg, grasping madly at the air before crashing heavily to the floor.

The three others landed on their knees beside him, all concern, till they saw his face was outraged, not pained, then they gave way to the most helpless laughter. He sat up, said in mock humiliation, 'It's going to serve you right, my dear brother-in-law, if I've slipped half a dozen discs and you have to inoculate all those sheep yourself. That child of yours will be the death of me! Such an undignified thing has never happened to me before.'

'No?' queried Emilie, with more honesty than tact. 'What about the time you tripped on the down escalator at the shop and hurled yourself at a glass showcase? It took fifteen stitches to put you together again, and a customer fainted and had to be sent home in a taxi!

Never mind, that laugh's done me good. But seriously, Hugh, you aren't hurt, are you?'

'A lot you care, really. The answer is, only in my pride. Right, let's get at our Scrabble. Have you got that turntable thing you ice the cakes on, to put the board across? Much easier than turning it manually.'

An hour and a half later Rosamond found herself thinking the slate really had been wiped clean, the hatchet buried ... oh, dear, all those clichés again! She giggled out loud, and they gazed at her in surprise and approval. 'You're laughing at your thoughts,' said Emilie delightedly. 'I like that. It sounded so natural. You've been so determined of late not to obtrude on our family circle I've been ready to scream. Are you going to tell us what you're laughing at?'

'It wouldn't be so funny to anyone else. It was just that Matthieu couldn't stop talking in clichés as we were walking up, and I found myself thinking in them just now.'

The tawny eyes searched her face. 'Same clichés? Or another set? I mean, about the same subject?'

Her colour deepened slightly. 'The very same,' she admitted.

'Good, then I'll add another ... it's going to be all plain sailing from now on.' They both laughed.

Rod went to say something, but Emilie put out a hand and stopped him. 'No, Rod, don't. They know what they're talking about and I've a feeling it's important, yet not for general issue. I'm going to make some coffee ... come and help me.'

Rod leaned back in his chair, stretching his legs out. 'No fear! If they've got things to say to each other, which I've suspected this long time past, they can damn well say them when they're going home. Doesn't take long enough to make coffee.'

'Oh, dear,' said Rosamond. 'In that case, Emilie, I'll help you get it. Though what privacy a room like this with the kitchen at one end would have given, I know not.' They all laughed and it was very pleasant, not strained.

As they drank their coffee and nibbled the delicious club sandwiches Emilie had prepared earlier, talk became general, mainly farming, with Rosamond feeling relaxed enough to ask question after question on matters of which she was as yet abysmally ignorant.

Rod said, 'Even after you've had a full year's cycle of the farming calendar here, Rosamond, you'll still be full of wonder, still find things to ask. The seasons and the weather change so, as well as farming techniques. I hope we'll show you a good lambing come October . . . we lamb late up here . . . but I wouldn't like you to experience a spring for your first up here like the one Elissa and Logan had. Though somehow, come to think of it, it solved all *their* differences.'

Matthieu, rather hurriedly, began to talk about the shop, mentioning the success of the fashion parade. To Rosamond's surprise he mentioned her part in it. Emilie, twinkling, said, 'And you tried to make us believe you were a very unimportant cog in the big business wheel, Rosamond.'

Rosamond decided not to take that up. 'I thought it was quite fascinating having an autumn showing in March. We had some lovely models. Emilie, you'd know Verna Halley, I suppose? She was ravishing with that lovely copper hair and her height and elegance. She ought to be a professional.'

'Except that she's too lazy by far,' said Matthieu. 'Pity there was never the necessity to earn her own living . . . when she was a teenager, I mean. I think the time's fast approaching when she might have to.'

Rosamond's voice held surprise. 'Really? But to visit their home you'd never dream of that.'

'You've never known such a spender as the mother—Cilla Halley. While the husband was alive he kept the brakes on. She spent wildly the first three or four years after he died—converted investments into cash, threw gay parties, took several trips to America. Oh, it's been ridiculous. She had an idea that the MacQueen business could recoup it for her. Poor Grandfather, the pace was really hot. Or do I mean the chase? That's really why he took this trip even if Pierre was still away.'

Rosamond knew a feathering of fear. What was he going to say? They were obsessed by this notion of the grandfather being pursued by females on the make. They wanted to keep the MacQueen money within the family fold. No wonder, when long ago, the family fortune had been willed away to a gold-digger. But she hoped he wasn't bringing this up to get at her again, was he? He'd just said they must bury the hatchet ... oh, dear, she was at it again!

Aggravatingly, he practically changed the subject and said, with the air of one just recollecting something, 'Oh, by the way, Rosamond, your grandmother rang here today.'

Her lips parted, she boggled at him. 'Gran? You mean from Canada? What——?'

He held up a finger, 'No, from Dunedin. She said you probably hadn't expected her to arrive so soon. I gather you knew she was planning a visit?'

'Yes, but—oh, surely they could have told me she was on the way. I'll ring her right now. Oh, what day is it? Wednesday ... they have a meeting Wednesdays. She's bound to be with them. She leaves us all standing the way she enters into everything. Matthieu, I——'

But he'd turned from her to Rod and Emilie. 'Has Rosamond told you yet that our grandfather and her grandmother were once sweethearts? I'd like to say lovers if you could use it in the good old-fashioned courting term that you find in out-of-date books. Because that was what they were.'

Emilie leaned forward. 'I know Rosamond thought her grandmother must have worked on this estate or one of the other lakeside ones. She thought it would have been within the view of Mount Serenity, because

Rosamond's aunt, her father's sister, is called Serena.
Go on, Matthieu. I'm loving this. But I take it they
parted and he married Grandma?'

'It was Grandma who parted them. She'd marked
him down for her own, so she told lies, and Grandfather married her on the rebound. Then, a long time
after Grandma had winkled him out of here and all he
loved, into the family business, she had a near fatal illness and confessed. It knocked Grandfather for six. I
don't know if you ever knew, Sis, I did, but not all of it
... he lost his memory for a few days. But he'd had a
reasonably good marriage and he had a family. Things
settled down. She was never quite so dictatorial again
... and he mellowed too.

'Grandfather thought he was seeing the young Louise
again when he met Rosamond Louise in England. He
brought her out here. He didn't know Louise was
widowed by now, and Rosamond wouldn't tell him because she had a vague idea that the love of Louise's life
was someone different, not a draper, but a farmer. Rosamond and I had a most unfortunate first meeting ...
in Southampton. My fault entirely. But some time after
she was catapulted into my life by our impulsive grand-
sire, we cleared that one up, or seemed to. Then ...
bingo! ... she departed the scene while I was in Australia, leaving no address.

'*No*, Rosamond!' he interrupted her. 'Hear me out. I
just want to put Rod and Emilie in the picture, then I'm
taking you outside and supposing I have to choke it out
of you, you're going to tell me what went wrong, because I just can't believe you don't—you didn't—well,
let that go. Rod's looking far too interested. Now,
here's something Emilie knows something about,
though I wasn't explicit with Emilie on the phone,
didn't have much time and was too conscious of the
fact that a shop phone is never private. I knew Cilla
Halley would never give up. I thought the only thing
would be to get Grandfather safely married to someone
else—I thought he just could succumb out of sheer

loneliness. So I wrote a letter to Rosamond's grandmother when I was in Australia, having got her address from Rosamond's mother, and simply said to Louise that I'd found out who our new fashion compere was, that Gaspard had imported her simply and solely because she was her living image, and was it possible for her to come to New Zealand, stay in Dunedin, and meet Gaspard again. That it would give him great joy. I said he had a lifelong regret that he had parted from her in anger because someone had made mischief, and would she give him this chance to make his peace with her? I dared not say more. That's over to them, but I can't believe that they won't spend their last years together ... and it would spike Cilla Halley's guns for ever. Rosamond, what did you say? Or at least what are you trying to say?'

In her complete amazement she stood up, swallowed, then said, 'Matthieu, then it wasn't *me* you were trying to stop marrying your grandfather ... marrying him for his money? You weren't just playing a game ... pretending you—Oh, Matthieu!'

He was on his feet too, staring, though they stood the distance apart that their chairs had been. For a long moment they held each other's eyes, the truth breaking through ...

Relief was succeeding the astonishment on Matthieu's face. He said, 'Rosamond, out with it! For God's sake don't let's have any more misunderstandings. *What* did you think?'

She gulped, said, 'The afternoon before you went to Australia I took some ads along to you. Shona got called out and asked me to type the last page of your report. When I was finished I heard you on the phone. I thought you were talking about *me*! You said I was definitely on the make, but that you'd save your grandfather from me. You said: "Remember how Grandfather saved Pierre from that girl? Well, this is it in reverse." What else could I think?'

Matthieu groaned. 'Go on ... ?'

'I was just going to Dunedin to try for a job there, but when I picked up the ads from your desk, I saw that one for a governess and came here.'

She'd never seen Matthieu look like this before. He might have his grandmother's features, but Ellie would never have looked like this. Not a hard line was left. Emilie and Rod had ceased to exist for him. All their future was in the look he gave her.

She said, 'Then it wasn't play-acting . . . it was for real?'

'It was for real,' he said simply.

In the ensuing silence neither of them knew quite what to say and into that silence came the sound of Rod rubbing his hands together in utter satisfaction. They both jerked their heads in his direction. Rod said: 'This is capital, capital! What a yarn this'll make to tell when I'm best man at your wedding. How many best men can actually boast that they were present at the very proposal?'

Matthieu grinned, took a threatening step towards him. 'If I thought you'd do that to me, I'd slit your throat here and now! If you think for one instant I'm going to have any witnesses when I actually ask Rosamond to marry me, you're sadly mistaken . . . there's a moon outside, and a lake . . .' He turned to Rosamond. 'Do you mind waiting, love?'

There were dancing lights in the velvety eyes, reflected from the firelight. 'I do mind, actually. I'd like to make quite sure of you in front of witnesses. I'll have you, Matthieu, if you still want me.'

'*If I want you!*' He took a step towards her, checked.

Rod groaned, 'I knew it . . . we're going to be done out of the final clinch . . . good grief, look at Emilie . . . what on earth's the matter with her?'

They gazed at her. Emilie's beautiful blue eyes, so like old Gaspard's, were thick with glittering tears. 'I'm so happy,' she sobbed, 'so happy . . . the moment I saw Rosamond I wanted her for Hugh. It's just too, too beautiful.'

They burst into laughter in which Emilie, finally, joined.

Rod sobered up, said, 'All right. We'll have to do the decent thing and lose you to that moon. Off with you!'

Surprisingly, Matthieu shook his head. 'It has to be postponed, though not for long. Louise is ringing at eleven.' He grinned, 'I was so fed up with the baffling change in Rosamond I made up my mind to get to the bottom of it tonight. Yes, I was as cocksure of the fact that she loved me as that! I woke in the small hours this morning convinced something was wrong that could be righted. But getting her to myself was another thing. So I cooked this up. The men must be wondering what's got into me. I jacked it up with one of them to ask me for cards in front of Rosamond.

'I thought if I could create a pleasant family atmosphere, then blaze off all my ammunition at her, she'd have to come out with the truth, seeing Rod and Emilie would be here. But I never even got to that point. I said that bit about Cilla, and Rosamond gave it all away. It was a slight complication to have her grandmother ring today, but I was glad I'd answered the phone. I think your mother has known more than she said all along, Rosamond,' he added. 'I'm sure she knew this was our property, but had the sense not to say so. I'm bucked your grandmother responded so quickly to my letter. She didn't commit herself on the phone, but I'm pretty sure she'll consent to seeing Grandfather. Look, come and sit on the couch with me and sort it all out. A few ends might need tying up. Not that I'll allow anything to affect the outcome.'

Her hand was in his. They sat close, laughing, sighing, exclaiming. Nothing mattered now. Matthieu said, 'I tried to be too clever and nearly goosed my own romance. I didn't want Cilla pestering my grandfather as soon as he returned, so I called and dropped a few hints that by now his money was well tied up, that he no longer had full control of it, hadn't for years. That it had been put into a Family Trust because he'd wanted

us to enjoy it in his lifetime, not when he was gone.
That a good deal of it has been ploughed back into
extending this estate and that most of the income from
the shop will, eventually, go to Pierre, as he shoulders
all the responsibility there.'

He grinned. 'I don't want to sound as if I think I'm
irresistible, but it set Verna off too. She told me I was a
fool for allowing it to be all tied up like that, that I'd
never make as much farming as in the rag trade, that in
farming, it was all sunk in the land and improvements,
that I ought to have played my cards better. I told her
the money was only secondary, that I had the life I
wanted.' He looked down on Rosamond. Her head was
against his shoulder. 'She was extremely catty about
you—said that there was a girl who couldn't stand me
. . . that you'd gone off to catch up with Jeffrey Vane.
Since coming here I've wondered, seeing that was
manifestly untrue, if she made any mischief at all. I was
going to ask you tonight, but your surprising reaction
when I mentioned Cilla Halley, and my plan for keeping her away from Grandfather, put it out of my mind.
Did she?'

Rosamond looked confused. He said, 'Come on . . . if
anything else remains in doubt, I want it cleared up.
Darling, don't let history repeat itself. The mischief
made all those years ago kept two people apart all their
lives . . .' then he looked startled, said, 'though come to
think of it, if it hadn't, there wouldn't have been me,
and there wouldn't have been you . . . what an appalling
thought! Rosamond, what did Verna say?'

'I'd better tell you, but if you can't explain it, it
doesn't matter. As we know so well, things taken out of
context can sound so damning. But it sort of confirmed
what you said on the phone.

'It was after you left for Australia. Verna came
round. My own attitude about you probably triggered
it off. I was pretending I didn't care tuppence for you.
She said you could be charming when it suited you, that
all the MacQueens thought themselves the targets of

fortune-hunters. To do her justice I don't think she had the ghost of an idea that the girl in question was me, but she said you'd got a scare when you went overseas, thought your grandfather was falling for someone young and that you had visions of having to stay to rescue him by making up to her yourself, then leaving her cold. But to your surprise, your grandfather had gone quite happily off to Russia. It added fuel to the fire as far as I was concerned, but—but if it's something hard to explain, all this time since, it doesn't matter.'

Matthieu's look was tender, if rueful, and dispelled poor Emilie's immediate anxiety. 'I can explain it. Talk about life and death in the power of the tongue! It serves me right, I was trying to be too clever. I'd got pressured into having a meal with the Halleys. Mrs Halley was going on as usual about my grandfather ... how lonely he must be and so on ... and I couldn't resist it. Said: "Loneliness my foot ... he's a gay old dog." Then she said pretty much what Verna repeated to you. It flashed into my mind and I used it. It must have sounded damning, to you.'

Rosamond said, 'What a fool I was to believe Verna! I ought to have realised that despite what she said, she was still jealous ... I ought to have stayed and had a showdown with you when you arrived back. Only I——' her eyes fell '—only I was afraid you'd guess I cared for you. Girls still feel like that, no matter how much our status has changed.'

He laughed. 'All my life I'll remember you suddenly appearing on the jetty at Glen Airlie ... and promptly disappearing into the lake!' He began to laugh. 'And you wouldn't even let me rescue you. Oh, I do wish your grandmother would ring.'

At that moment the telephone sounded. He took Rosamond with him to the phone. The other two unashamedly pricked their ears, sitting bolt upright. They heard Matthieu answer it confidently, then, '*Grandfather?* Good heavens ... you're ringing from Christchurch, of course? How strange, we were waiting for a

ring from Dunedin . . . what? You're in Dunedin? What
did you say? Staying at the Manse? No, I'm not going
deaf, sorry . . . I'll stop bawling in your ear. It's just
that . . . Grandfather, what *is* going on? Is Rosamond's
grandmother still there? I mean I—all right, I'll shut
up.'

It was too much for Emilie and Rod, they rushed
across and crowded as near the instrument as they
could. Matthieu held it a little away from his ear so that
Rosamond at last could get every word.

Gaspard's voice sounded ten years younger. 'Thank
you, Matthieu, for writing to Louise and suggesting she
should visit New Zealand. Nice to know it has your
approval. But I beat you by nearly a week. I called back
at Boston, from England, to see Pierre and Natalie, and
while there looked up the Vancouver directory, and
found no Professor Briarley in it, only a Mrs Briarley. I
rang her, found she was indeed a widow, asked if I
could come to see her. I swore Pierre and Natalie to
secrecy.

'We had a great week in Vancouver. We saw a lot of
scenery together, but also recaptured the years that the
locusts had eaten. She stopped off at Christchurch on
her way here, and she and Goldie took to each other at
once.' He cleared his throat. 'We're getting wed next
week. My new stepson-to-be—Rosamond's father—will
be tying the knot. We have it all planned. We're honey-
mooning at Te Anau as we planned long ago, and
spending a week at Strathdearn with you after that. We
want you all here for the wedding. Pierre and Natalie
and the Humphreys are coming down. How's that for
romance? By the way, Louise is by my side, and we
want to know something. She told me you said when
she rang this afternoon that if she rang at eleven, you
hoped to be able to tell her you and Rosamond were
engaged . . . you've taken a devil of a time about it,
young Matthieu . . . are you?'

Matthieu burst out laughing. 'We're not all speed
fiends like you, you old sinner, but yes, history *had* re-

peated itself, Grandfather, and mischief *had* been made, but tonight I bludgeoned her into telling me all. She's here with me, looking ravishing in rose-coloured velvet, with trimmings of white fur ... a creation from Mac-Queen's, no less ... I'll owe you a debt all my life for finding her for me ... Rosamond, say hullo to your new grandfather!'

She took the phone, said, 'But you'll always be Gaspard to me, darling.'

It was all of an hour before they parted from Emilie and Rod. It was midnight's witching hour. The Milky Way above the lake had surely never been so thickly encrusted with stars! Mount Serenity had never seemed so serene, so perfectly symmetrical, a fairy mountain, brooding over eternal snows with its silver radiance.

Matthieu and Rosamond took their way along the rock path, that led from the terraces towards the lindens and the murmuring pines. Ahead of them lay the homestead where, in just a matter of weeks, they would occupy a shared bedroom where once Margot and Angus MacQueen had slept together, made love, the room where Gaspard had been born, where Emilie had been born ... the piney path led, in turn, to that old garden where, in the years to come, their own children would play, but for their enchanted hour they were content to stay under the balsamy trees, shut into a world of their own.

The moon, shining through the branches on to the bleached lake-sand track, gave them enough light to see each other's faces, to read the looks in each other's eyes ... now full of trust and understanding.

Matthieu's fingers lingered on the jet bracelet on Rosamond's wrist, on the necklace at her throat, then his mouth came down on hers and thereafter was silence for a long, long time.

ATTRACTIVE, SPACE SAVING BOOK RACK

Display your most prized novels on this handsome and sturdy book rack. The hand-rubbed walnut finish will blend into your library decor with quiet elegance, providing a practical organizer for your favorite hard-or soft-covered books.

Only $9.95

Approximately 16" x 8" when assembled

Assembles in seconds!

To order, rush your name, address and zip code, along with a check or money order for $10.70 ($9.95 plus 75¢ postage and handling) (New York residents add appropriate sales tax), payable to *Harlequin Reader Service* to:

In the U.S.

Harlequin Reader Service
Book Rack Offer
901 Fuhrmann Blvd.
P.O. Box 1325
Buffalo, NY 14269-1325

Offer not available in Canada.

Here's how to get this special offer from Harlequin!

November
BETTY NEELS TREASURY EDITION COUPON

As simple as 1...2...3!

1. **Each month, save one Treasury Edition coupon from your favorite Romance or Presents novel.**
2. **In four months you'll have saved four Treasury Edition coupons (only one coupon per month allowed).**
3. **Then all you have to do is fill out and return the order form provided, along with the four Treasury Edition coupons required and $2.95 for postage and handling.**

Mail to: Harlequin Reader Service

In the U.S.A.	In Canada
901 Fuhrmann Blvd.	P.O. Box 609
P.O. Box 1397	Fort Erie, Ontario
Buffalo, NY 14240	L2A 9Z9

BN-Nov-2

Please send me my Special copy of the Betty Neels Treasury Edition. I have enclosed the four Treasury Edition coupons required and $2.95 for postage and handling along with this order form. (Please Print)

NAME_____

ADDRESS_____

CITY_____

STATE/PROV._____ ZIP/POSTAL CODE_____

SIGNATURE_____
This offer is limited to one order per household.

SUPPLIES LIMITED

This special Betty Neels offer expires
February 28, 1987.

Take 4 novels and a surprise gift FREE